The Mystery of Sarah Slater

Betty J. Vaughn

TotalRecall Publications, Inc.
1103 Middlecreek
Friendswood, Texas 77546
281-992-3131   281-482-5390 Fax
www.totalrecallpress.com

ISBN: 9781648830266
UPC: 643977402660
Library of Congress Control Number: 2020942369

Printed in the United States of America with simultaneous printings in Australia, Canada, and United Kingdom.

FIRST EDITION
1   2   3   4   5   6   7   8   9   10

To the mysterious woman who has captured the imagination of many, the vanished Sarah Slater. I hope I have treated her fairly as I have attempted to live through these turbulent times with her.

Betty!! You write one suspenseful thriller right after another!! It is difficult for an author to capture my attention to the extent that I do not want to stop reading, but you have succeeded in doing that!! I am in awe of your talent!! These books would make wonderful movies that would keep the audience on the edge of their seats. Some enterprising movie producer should buy the rights from you and put these 21st Century action/adventure books on the big screen!

--Dr. Judith Gordon

The author has a real gift for putting the reader "in the moment" and the scene of the narrative. She has the ability to move quickly from one scene to another when danger, suspense, or plain-old curiosity demands it. This author really knows how to drive a plot.

--Dr. Linda Hobson,
    Professor Emeritus of English, UNC, Chapel Hill, NC

Author's Note

Sarah Gilbert Slater fascinated me from the first moment I learned of her. I have long wanted to tell her story, despite the fact so much is unknown and so much is supposition. After extensive research through available documents, both online and in print, I have concluded it is best to leave the mystery an enigma.

As with any book, where so much has been lost to the mists of time or to deliberate obfuscation, the author must resort to poetic license to bring the story to life. While I have adhered to the few documented facts that exist, I have filled in the gaps for that period of her life that provide some vague outline. Hopefully, the assumptions I have made to fill in the gaps are reasonable given the parameters of time and known operatives. Unlike others who have written about the elusive Sarah, I refuse to make the leap to resolution of the mystery after she vanished from history in April 1865. I remain unconvinced by the theories presented in various articles when so much is based on errors, nor did I choose to invent a fictional life for Sarah after 1865. At the end of the book, I will cite where I have taken liberties, where I have adhered to documented facts, and where there are discrepancies in the proposed theories of what became of Sarah.

As in bringing any book to fruition, there are many to whom an author owes gratitude. I am grateful to Bruce Moran, my publisher, who believes in me and brings my books to print.

I am grateful to my editor and friend since our early teens, Dr. Judith Conway Gordon, who corrects my errors and makes my manuscript better through her recommendations.

My husband, Marty Atwater, reads each chapter as I write and makes corrections and suggestions as I go along. His insight has been invaluable as he is meticulous in his evaluation of the evolving plot. He is also responsible for creating the maps used in my novels and for the PowerPoint presentations I use in book signings.

My sister, Helen Johnson Brumbaugh, also read the completed manuscript and provided suggestions prior to the official editing by Dr. Gordon.

Jim Hodges, President of the New Bern Historical Society provided useful information on the New Bern Academy as well as photographs from Nineteenth Century New Bern. *Note: in the book, I adhered to the spelling of both New Bern (New Berne) and Goldsboro (Goldsborough) during the mid-1800's.*

Jane Gradeless Phillips was helpful in locating the site of the Campbell house in Kinston on the corner of Bright and Independence Streets. Jane is active in various historical societies in the Kinston area and has written numerous articles relative to Kinston's history.

A special thanks is owed to Rozalia Ghebhardt, costume maker extraordinaire who was gracious enough with her time and talent to make widow's weeds appropriate to the period, pose in them, and allow the photograph to be used on the cover. It is amazing the friends we meet on Facebook in all parts of the world. Rozalia, a native of Romania, now resides in Melbourne, Australia.

Through Rozalia I met another Facebook friend, Jane Clancy, her prize-winning photographer who was gracious enough to lend her artistry in capturing the images of Rozalia for the cover and text illustrations of Sarah. They are both two amazingly talented women who have gone beyond kindness in doing this for me. It is my hope that someday we will meet face to face, rather than through online posts.

I send a thank you to the McCord Museum in Montreal that generously allowed me to use the photo of the St. Lawrence Hall Hotel, to the Library of Congress, and others that have made photos accessible.

I must also thank Colleen Puterbaugh of the James O. Hall Research Center at the Surratt House Museum (a division of the Maryland-National Capital Park and Planning Commission,) for permission to use the photographs of the Surratt properties and for the article by John Stanton published in the Surratt Society Courier of March, 2016.

Image of Sarah Slater
courtesy of Rozalia Ghebbhardt model and dressmaker,
Copyrighted photo courtesy of Jane Clancy.

Contents

Maps

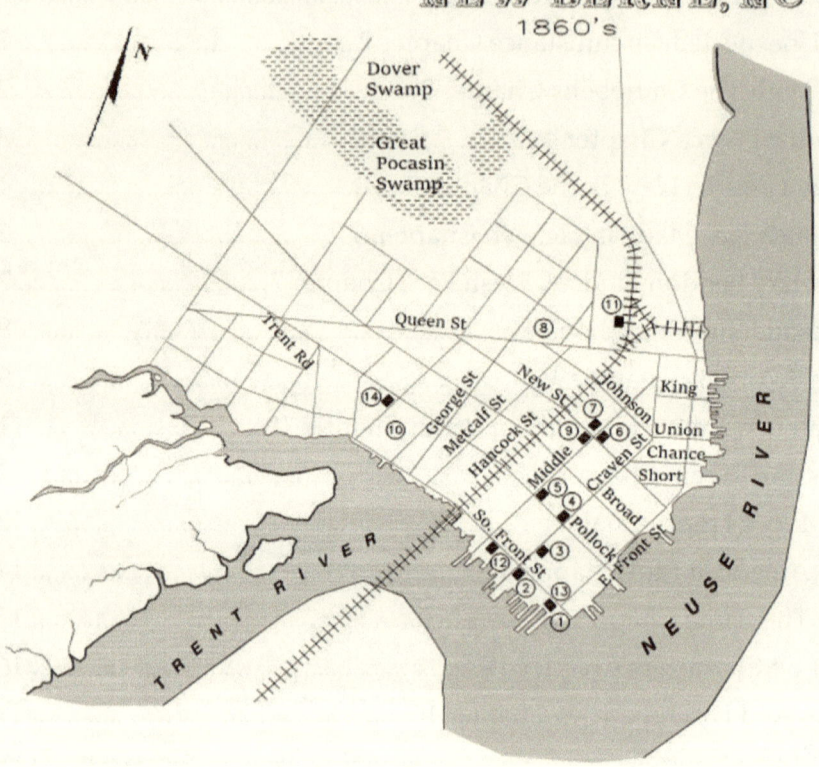

NEW BERNE, NC
1860's

LEGEND

① Union Point
② Harvey Mansion
③ Isaac Taylor House
④ City Hall/Post Office
⑤ Christ Episcopal Church
⑥ First Presbyterian Church
⑦ New Berne Academy

⑧ Cedar Grove Cemetary
⑨ John Wright Stanly House
⑩ Tryon Palace Grounds
⑪ Railroad Station
⑫ Gaston House Hotel
⑬ Laroque Office and Warehouses
⑭ Jones House (JAIL)

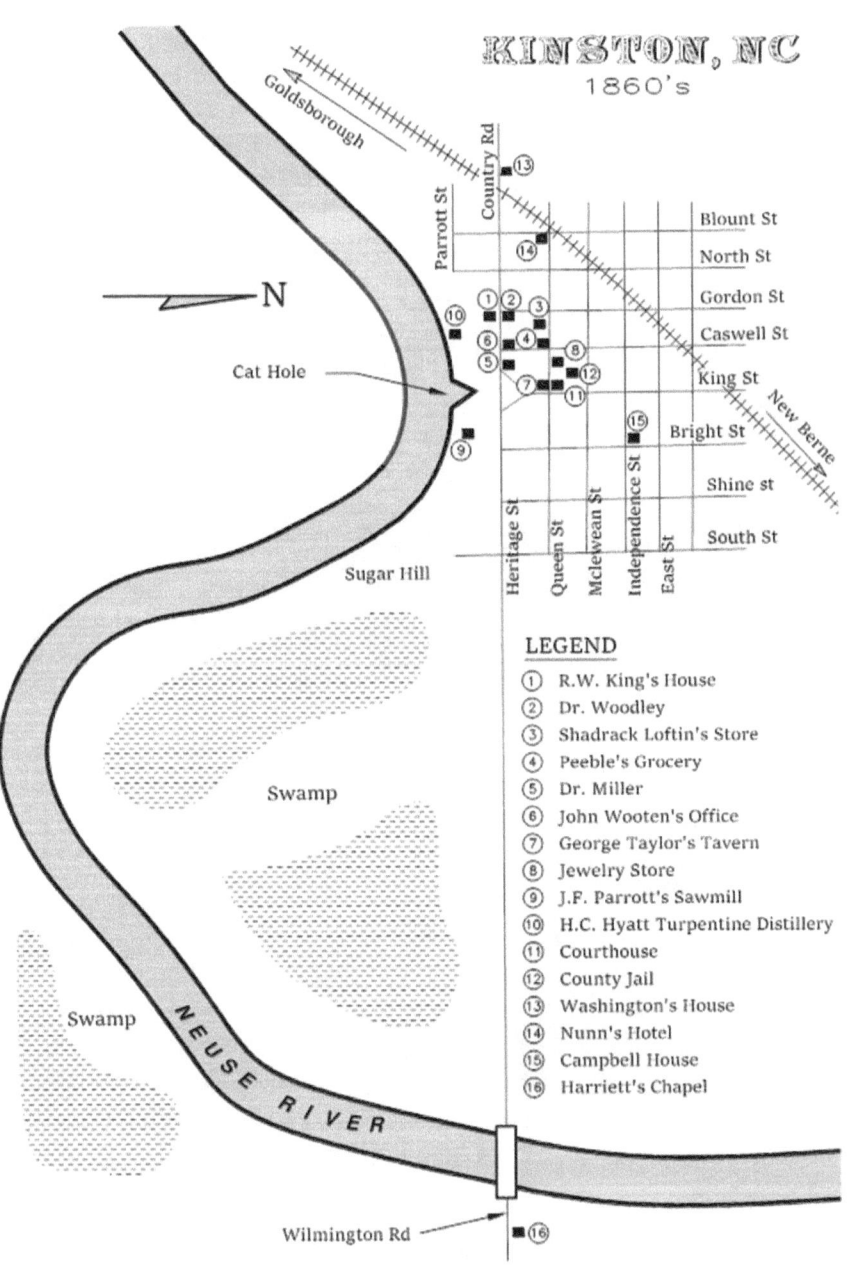

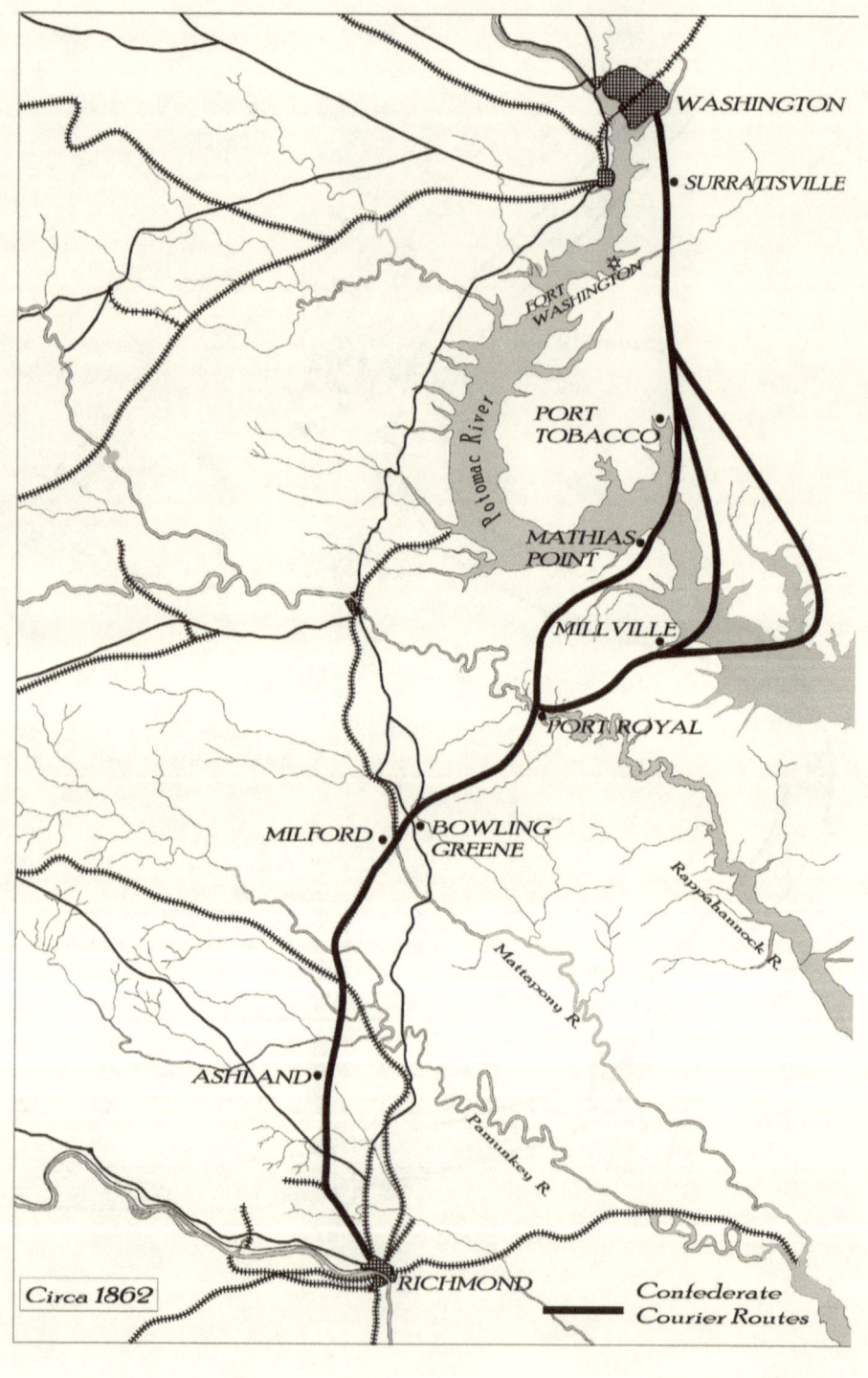

WASHINGTON

SURRATTSVILLE

FORT WASHINGTON

Potomac River

PORT TOBACCO

MATHIAS POINT

MILLVILLE

PORT ROYAL

MILFORD

BOWLING GREENE

Rappahannock R.

Mattapony R.

ASHLAND

Pamunkey R.

Circa 1862

RICHMOND

Confederate
Courier Routes

Foreword: Sarah's Message

I laugh at you all...all of you. You all thought you were so smart, but that is to my advantage. Did you think I tricked you or outsmarted you when I ran to save myself? You tried to destroy my very spirit, but you did not. Yes, I'm pretty and I'm clever...clever enough to be able to leave all this war and fighting behind and find a new life, one that you funded. You will never know me, but you will try. I have escaped your boundaries and have found my own. My real life lay ahead; and you will ponder me for decades, indeed centuries beyond me. I have touched the lives of greatness while my own is obscure. For me that is better. Otherwise, you might have hanged me along with another innocent woman. I have no desire to meet that fate, one that no other besides her has ever met in this land of noble ideals. How could any woman in a society so ruled by men do what I have done? I never planned this life, this path I have taken. Yet now, somehow, I want you to know a bit of my history. Perhaps, it will intrigue you. Am I a thief? Some would say I am. But then what is their measurement of reality, of life? Others will say I am an opportunist, cold and calculating. I defy your definitions and judgments unless you have lived the life that I have. Don't you see, I merely dared to seize the moment and make it mine.

MISERY IN HARTFORD
Chapter 1

Sarah was angry. It was January 12, 1860, and they were supposed to be celebrating her seventeenth birthday. It should have been a happy family gathering. She laughed at herself. How many of those had she known that had been happy, and why should this be any different?

Hartford, Connecticut

She looked across the table at her mother. Miserable in the early months of pregnancy, Antionette was glowering at her husband, Joseph Gilbert. As usual, they were arguing. Sarah could not image how they had stopped long enough to make another baby. Her brothers Robert and Frederick studiously ignored their parents.   Two years younger, Frederick had delighted in being a nuisance to Sarah. Six years older than Sarah, Robert was her favorite. Recently, he had opened a dentist office on Market Street and was helping to relieve some of the financial pressures on the family. Not that he received any gratitude from his parents. Nor did she receive recognition for her daily toil. Sarah could not suppress a sigh. The elder Gilberts were too preoccupied with quarreling to bother thanking their children for any help they provided. The only one missing was her older brother, Eugene, who, having had enough of the family drama, moved to Kinston, N.C., in 1858, where he was working as a jeweler.

The family was not prospering. They had moved from Middletown to Hartford, Connecticut, in 1858 after living in Middletown for eighteen years following her parents move from Martinique. While living in Middletown, the hapless Joseph scratched out a living teaching his native French language and manufacturing pills. Grandly, he labeled himself a doctor. The move to Hartford two years prior had brought no improvement in their circumstances. Their clapboard boarding house at 13 Sheldon Street provided a living, thanks to Sarah and her mother's cooking and cleaning. Her mother resented it. Sarah despised it.

They had fed the boarders early, so the family could celebrate her birthday without strangers. The cake Sarah had made for herself was sitting on the sideboard waiting for the meal to finish. There would have been no cake had she not made it, and there would be no gifts. There never had been.

She was young, beautiful of face and figure, and smart. Sarah felt she deserved more. Somehow, she was determined to find a better life, one that did not require her to toil like a slave and age early into a wrinkled, bitter prune like her mother. She could tell from the portrait of her mother and father, painted in more prosperous days, they had been a handsome couple. One that appeared to be in love.

Sarah was so deep in her thoughts that she did not at first note the raised volume of her father's voice. Looking up from her plate of mostly untouched food, she saw that he had risen from the table.

His face red with rage, Joseph exploded, "Dammit, Antionette. I can't take any more of your constant carping. I've had it."

"Really, so what are you going to do about it?" she demanded.

Joseph leaned across the table to glare at her mother. "Do? You think I have no other option but to take this day after day. Nothing I do is ever good enough for you. What don't you try figuring it out on your own? I'm leaving."

"That's just like you. You fill my belly with a baby for the tenth time and now you want to run off. I've buried five of them and now there is another on the way. It nearly broke my heart when my babies died, and not a word of sympathy from you. You never stopped to consider my pain. You have never stopped to consider me, period. Now, you want to leave me like this, you bastard." Antoinette glared back at her husband. "So, get out. Go! I've had enough of you. Leave me to raise a fatherless babe. He'll be better off without the likes of you."

Joseph was so angry he sputtered. "What the hell are you talking about? I loved those babies and grieved for them as much as you did. That never mattered to you. You are the only one you care about. The rest of us be damned."

The three siblings looked at one another. Their parents had

fought before, but never had it reached this point. Sarah could not help trembling. What would they do if their father left? It was hard enough to survive with all of them working. Sarah and her brothers quietly left the room and the uncut cake behind. None had any appetite.

Sarah shrugged her shoulders when Robert looked at her as though questioning what she thought would happen. Going to her room, she shed her clothes and pulled her nightgown over her head. She climbed into the bed and nestled under the feather covering until her shivering stopped. Normally she would have wrapped a hot brick to slide under the covers and warm her feet, but the need to escape the quarrel still raging downstairs had been too great. Staring at the fading floral wallpaper, Sarah mindlessly counted the roses until the candle guttered out plunging the room into darkness. With her mind in turmoil, sleep was elusive due to intermittent bouts of shouting from her father and crying and screaming from her mother. She suspected none in the house were sleeping, including the boarders. If things continued in this vein, the boarders would leave, and then where would they be?

At four in the morning her father knocked on her door. Sarah struggled to awaken before mumbling, "What is it?"

Joseph stuck his head in the door. "Sarah, I'm going to Kinston to join Eugene. If you want to go with me, get packed and be downstairs in an hour. Fred is coming, too. Don't worry about packing everything. Robert will ship the rest to you when we are settled."

"Robert is not going with you?"

"No. He is going to stay with your mother until after the baby is born in June. Then he's coming, as well."

"What about maman?"

"She says she will sell the house and move to New York. Her cousin there will help her get settled." Joseph cleared his throat, "If you're coming with us, get a move on so we don't miss the train."

Sarah lay back on the bed. What was she to do? To stay meant on-going toil, even more poverty, and her mother's slaps and verbal abuse. While she knew nothing of Kinston, a small town in eastern North Carolina, it at least promised something new…maybe something better. For a moment she felt pity for her mother with a husband abandoning her and a baby due in months. But, she reasoned, Antoinette had brought much of the trouble on herself with the constant carping and degrading of not only her husband, but her children as well. Sarah and her father had borne the brunt of it. With the others gone, were she to stay, it would be Robert and her that were the focus of her mother's eternal wrath. But, she would be the primary target. Sarah sat up. There was no time to waste, if she was going…and she was. Anything was better than this. She would miss Robert, but he would come later.

Dressing hastily and throwing her clothes helter-skelter into her battered valise, she was out the door of her room and downstairs at five minutes to the appointed hour. Frederick and her father were waiting. Robert was there, too. Judging by the shine in his eyes, he was struggling to hold back tears. She suspected he already regretted his decision to stay. Sarah looked around the dimly lit foyer, but her mother was nowhere in sight.

Walking over to Robert, she dropped her valise to the floor and stepped into his arms. "I'll miss you. If it gets too bad, you come to Kinston, too."

"It's okay." Robert added in a voice meant for just her ear, "I'm not happy about it, but someone needs to stay with mother until after the baby. It's just not right for us all to leave her like this. Papa deserves some of the blame for this mess, Nettie." Robert always called her by the family nickname.

Annoyed by the whispering that he suspected reflected poorly on him, Joseph reminded, "Enough chatter, we need to get going now,"

Sarah stepped back from Robert, squeezed his hand and whispered she loved him. Her only answer was a nod and a sad smile. Of all in her family, she loved this brother of hers best. She studied him as though to memorize his features. Robert was handsome in a quiet way. His slim but manly stature, azure blue eyes, and a head-full of curly hair had drawn many admiring glances from the female sex. For Sarah, his best attribute was a kind and loving heart.

"I'll write you," she called back as the three of them walked into the cold dark of early morning.

Her father and Fred sat across from her in the train. Sarah was relieved that they had found a seat near the coal-fed stove. While it nearly blistered her face, they were better off than those passengers relegated to the cold rear of the car. Her valise was beside her on the seat. Laying the book that she had packed at the last minute on top of the bag, and pulling her best paisley shawl over her face, she leaned back and closed her eyes. She had slept little during the night and felt ill and out of sorts due to the lack of rest. The rhythmic clacking of the train lulled her into sleep as the miles slipped past. She awakened with a jolt as they pulled into the station in New York where they would change trains for the next stage of the journey south.

Sarah and Frederick both gawked at the swarms of people whirling about in the station. Their previous experiences had never exposed them to such a bustling city as New York. As she stared around, she saw a handsome man, that looked to be in his early twenties, admiring her. Sarah could not resist a flirtatious smile in return.

Catching her, Joseph jerked her around by the elbow. "Enough of that, Sarah Antoinette Gilbert. I'll not have you acting like some strumpet. You hear me now."

In sham meekness, Sarah bowed her head and murmured, "Yes, Papa."

To say anything more would only increase his smoldering anger from the night before. She did not want to spend the rest of the journey listening to him harangue her for her comportment. For a moment, she wondered if leaving with her father was the best decision after all. Sarah sighed under her breath. There was no turning back now. Frederick, for once, gave her a sympathetic glance. He was as wary as she of their father's anger in his present mood. It was a relief to them both to follow their father to the train that would carry them to Washington, and then on to Richmond where they would again change trains.

As she walked behind Joseph, she could not help wondering what had become of the handsome, proudly erect man that stood beside her mother in the portrait that hung over the fireplace in the parlor. In the intervening years, her father had become gray-headed, with a face lined by a myriad of creases. He stooped as if the burden of living was too heavy a weight on his sagging shoulders. The smile that lit the face in the portrait had been replaced by a perpetual glower as though the eyes that looked out at the world saw no hope. Her once beautiful mother's eyes had that same look of despair, frustration, and dead dreams. Was it life that had wrought such changes, or was it blaming their despair on each other and losing hope for anything better? In their anger, they had pulled against one another rather than joining forces to fight for a more promising future. Sarah had decided, before sleep claimed her that last night in her home, never to allow their failures and frustrations to consume her own life. With the sun just beginning to peak from behind a cloud, it seemed as though it was sending her a ray of hope.

They settled themselves on the ubiquitously hard slat seats of the next train and tried to find a comfortable posture. They were all eager to reach Washington and stop for some rest.

When they arrived in Washington, they exited the train to grab a bite to eat from the kiosk inside the station. The overly salted ham and stale bread was unappealing, but they ate without complaining as they were all hungry and exhausted from the long day of travel. Sarah suspected that any accommodation they could find for the night would be, at best, a nearby rooming house…one that her father could afford.

Her father made inquiries inside the wooden depot building, and soon the three of them were trudging down the street to an inauspicious looking dwelling. Knocking on the door, they waited until a slovenly woman answered Joseph's knock and motioned for them to come in. The best the woman could offer was a single room. Her father and brother would share the bed while she was consigned to a pallet on the floor. She was too tired to care. The woman fed them a spare breakfast of oatmeal in the morning that they all ate in haste, washing it down with weak coffee. Brushing the clothing she had worn since leaving

Hartford, the characteristically well-groomed Sarah realized that achieving any semblance of freshness to her attire was a lost cause.

When they returned to the ramshackle station, Joseph telegraphed Eugene to tell him they were coming to Kinston and to book a hotel room for them. Then he purchased sandwiches for the next leg of the journey. He bought beer for himself and water for his children. Neither Sarah nor Fred commented on the beer. Sarah hoped it was enough to put him to sleep so she could escape his constant eyes on her as he watched for any further infraction of his strict code of what constituted proper behavior for his daughter. He was worse than the nuns that had overseen her education with an ever-ready ruler.

She was thrilled when he finally nodded off, leaving her to enjoy the scenery slipping past the window in quiet contemplation. Never having been anywhere except Hartford and Middletown, she found herself fascinated by the changing vista. In a low voice to keep from waking her father, she pointed out various views that captured her interest. Frederick, caught between the exuberance of childhood and the restraint of early adulthood, was as excited as she by the varied landscape although he tried to temper his enthusiasm in order to appear more mature.

When they arrived at the Richmond depot, they again changed trains as the gaslights came on inside the station. This leg of the journey would take them to Weldon, North Carolina, just over the Virginia border. In Weldon, they would transfer to the Wilmington and Weldon Railroad that would carry them to Goldsborough where they would catch the final train to their destination. With money tight, the senior Gilbert opted for the night train rather than spending the night in a hotel.

As night descended, the three of them nodded in weariness as their railcar carried them through the darkness. They roused enough when they reached Weldon to once again gather their things and transfer to the next train that stood puffing out black smoke against the moonlit sky of early dawn. In annoyance, Sarah brushed at the cinders that sifted down on her clothes. It was bad enough to look wrinkled and weary without adding dirt to the mix.

Resettled on the train, Sarah shifted on the hard seat trying to get comfortable. Falling back to sleep appeared to be a lost cause, so she sat up and resumed staring out at the gray of dawning day. From time to time she stomped her feet to try to get warm as they had not been lucky enough to get seats near the stove. After whistle stops in Halifax and Enfield, they pulled into the station in Rocky Mount. She watched three people detrain and walk into the depot, but no one got on. The small town beyond the shack-like depot was dark with only the roofs and trees standing in relief against the rosy sky of early morning. In minutes they left the station. She knew from the train schedule they had been given that the next stop was Wilson and then Goldsborough. There they would change to the Atlantic and North Carolina Railroad. They were all stiff and ready to get off when the conductor announced Goldsborough.

Walking to the train that would take them to their final destination, they stood waiting to board under the shelter of a small covered area on the platform. The day was gray with a fine drizzle that added to the general gloom of the scene. Goldsborough, despite being a juncture of two railroad lines, was a small town. Sarah hoped Kinston would be larger and offer a more appealing place to live. Nearby stood several men who, according to their conversation, were traveling to their home in New Bern. Her brother overheard them calling the train The Old Mullet Line. Curious, he approached them and stood waiting for them to notice him. The oldest of the men, clad in working man's clothing, turned.

Taking the opening, Fred asked, "Excuse me, sir. I just heard you call this The Old Mullet Line. We thought it was the Atlantic and North Carolina Railroad. That's the one we need."

The man chuckled, "Right enough, sonny. That's the official name, but local folks call it The Old Mullet Line because it hauls fish from the coast when it's coming from the other direction. If you ride near the freight car they haul'em in, you'll soon know what I mean. They can't get the stink of fish out of that thing." Again, he chuckled before spitting a stream of brown liquid off to the side.

Fred stared at the man as he wiped his mouth with the back of his hand. "What was that you just spat, sir?"

He laughed, showing brown stained teeth before responding, "Well, if your northern brogue ain't enough to give it away, that question sure does. It was snuff. You ever hear of that?"

"No, sir. What is it?"

"It's ground up tobacco. You put a pinch in your mouth and let'er rest. 'Bout everyone 'round here dips."

"Thank you, sir."

"Anytime." The man glanced back at Sarah and Joseph who were motioning for Fred to come back so they could board. "We're going to be on this train for a while. You get tired of settin' with your folks, come over and I'll tell you all about where you're going. By the way, where are y'all going?"

"Kinston. My brother lives there."

"Yup. Know the town right well. Got some kinfolk there."

"Yes, sir. Thank you again, sir.

When he rejoined his family, Joseph asked, "What are you doing talking to those

strangers?"

"Just asking about the train, Papa. He said he knows Kinston and can tell us a little about it while we are on the train."

"You don't need to go talking to strange folks. Your brother can tell us what we need to know when we get to Kinston."

"Yes, Papa."

Fred and his siblings all called their father papa, using the French pronunciation. Joseph's father had married a woman from Martinique, and they had raised their family on the island. Their mother was born in Trinidad. Both of their parents had grown up speaking French. In the Gilbert home much of the conversation was in French, so their children had grown up fluent in both French and English. Sarah did not know it then, but one day the dual languages would prove to be an asset.

Sarah, her father, and brother were a weary trio when they reached the Kinston station. Only twenty-five miles from Goldsborough and with no stops along the way, it had proven to be a mercifully short trip. Looking out the window, she saw the late afternoon sky was still weeping. Her brother was huddled by the station, looking wet and miserable. Despite that, she saw him straighten up and smile when the train stopped. For the first time, she noted his strong resemblance to Joseph's portrait.

AN UNEXPECTED CIRCUMSTANCE
Chapter 2

Walking down the muddy street as they left the station, Sarah's heart sank. The town was mostly wooden dwellings, many unpainted. Frederick met her eye and shook his head. It was obvious he was none too impressed either. Joseph ignored them as he strode ahead with Eugene who had always been his favorite. Hurrying to catch up, she heard Eugene telling her father that the population of the town was just over 1,300, the county of Lenoir about 11,000, of which half were slaves. Sarah, accustomed to growing up in Connecticut where slavery was considered a scourge on the country, shuddered at the thought of fifty percent of the human beings in this new home living in bondage. Her father, having grown up in the Caribbean where slavery was an established part of the economy, did not have her same compunctions.

Eugene went on to brag about the fresh air with few smoking factories to pollute it, the clean water from artesian wells, the booming carriage trade, and the products of the local agrarian community: pork, peas, sweet potatoes, tobacco, cotton, lumber, turpentine, tar, rye, and wheat. Transportation to the port and market hub of New Bern, thirty miles away, was by shipping on flat bottom scows perfect for navigating the muddy Neuse River, or by the railroad that had brought them from Goldsborough. With the completion of the railroad in 1858, he explained that Kinston was beginning to boom. However, Sarah could not help but wonder how he made a living making jewelry in such a modest community. When her father asked about it, Eugene explained that there were a number of wealthy people in the county and even some of the poorer citizens frequented him for simple gold wedding bands, lockets, brooches, watches, and various other items.

House near Neuse River Bridge, Kinston

She dropped back to walk beside Fred. She had heard enough to wonder how Eugene liked the town so much despite all the things he listed and saw as positives. Leaving one of the largest cities in the country with a population of over 27,000, Sarah could only shudder. Hartford was a prosperous manufacturing city with the amenities that she had come to expect. She could not help but wonder how her father, Fred, and she were to survive. She doubted there would be much demand for the French lessons Joseph had given in Hartford. His useless pills might be marketable to a gullible local population, but could they survive on that? As for herself, she possessed excellent academic skills, sang and played the piano with rare ability, and could teach French better than her father; but the only work experience she had was occasionally filling in for her mother in giving music lessons and helping her mother run a boarding house. Her heart sank at the thought of once again toiling away at that kind of labor. Then, she remembered. Surely, slaves were doing that kind of work here. So, what was to become of her? For the first time, she was truly sorry she had left home with her father.

Her thoughts were interrupted by Eugene informing them they would be staying at the Nunn Hotel on Blount Street where he had a room. Her father would share a room with Fred and Eugene. Thankfully, she realized she would have her own room. That seemed to be the only bright spot in the day.

The next morning dawned clear and crisp. The three newcomers walked with Eugene to his jewelry shop on Queen Street. On the way, on the right side of the street they passed Peeble's Grocery, and the two largest shops. Eugene told them as they ambled along that the first belonged to Shadrack Loftin and the second to R. W. King, both prominent members of the community. In front of King's shop, they crossed the street to Eugene's small shop beside the county jail. On the other side of the jail was the county courthouse. They left him there and continued down Queen Street to the corner where they turned right onto King Street. Originally named Kingston, following the Revolutionary War, the patriotic citizens dropped the 'g' as an act of rebellion and renamed the town Kinston. They never got around to changing the names of King and Queen Streets. As they rounded the corner, Joseph spotted the sign for George Taylor's Tavern. Telling Sarah and Frederick to go on back to the hotel, he went into the tavern.

When he joined them for the noon meal back at the hotel, he informed Frederick, that beginning the next day, the two of them would be working at Hyatt's turpentine factory on the banks of the river just off Heritage Street. He mentioned he had met Hyatt and M. W. Campbell in the tavern.

Lumber Company, Neuse River, Kinston

Turning to Sarah, he put his fork on his plate, and said, "You need to go to your room and pack after lunch. You will be staying with Mr. Campbell where you will be a governess for his children. I told him you could teach letters, numbers, music, French, and whatever else they might require. You make sure you do a good job. We can't all afford to live in this hotel. With me and your brothers working, it will be all we can do to take care of ourselves."

Sarah pushed her plate away and stood up. Without saying a word, she turned on her heel and marched from the dining room. She climbed the stairs, stomping on every step. Obviously, her father had no intention of them staying together as a family, and she was the most expendable. First, he abandoned his pregnant wife, and now he was abandoning her. When she reached her room, her anger had given away to tears that began to run down her cheeks. Dashing them away with her hand, she opened her door and dragged her valise from under the bed. She would not let her father see how he had hurt her. She would not go down with a tear-stained, swollen face. As far as she was concerned, Monday, January 17, 1860, was the day she disowned her father.

It did not take her long to pack the few things she had brought, leave the room, and return to the dining room where Frederick and her father were finishing their meal. She could tell by Fred's face that he was angry with their father, as well. Eugene would not meet her eyes as he excused himself from the table and left. Neither did Joseph look up when he shoved a scrap of paper to her without comment.

Sarah picked it up and stared at the address and the directions written on it. Sarah struggled for a moment to mask her emotions, then asked, "Fred, would you mind walking me to Mr. Campbell's house?"

"Sure, Nettie. I don't want you walking alone in a strange town."

Neither Fred nor Sarah looked back as they left Joseph sitting alone at the table. Sarah heard her father belch rudely just as they reached the door of the room. She did not care if she ever saw him again.

For the first couple of blocks, they walked without talking. Finally, Fred burst out, "I don't know which of our parents is more selfish. All they ever think about is themselves, first and foremost. I can't believe he is making you go live with people you have never even met. Then he goes and hires me out without even considering what I might like to do. I'm almost fifteen years old. Old enough for him to begin treating me like a man and not some boy he can order around. I don't want to work in some turpentine factory. I bet there are plenty of other jobs around if I could have just asked about them."

"You won't have much choice tomorrow. But, in the next few weeks, maybe you can look around and find something else to do. I certainly intend to find something. If I don't, I'll save what I earn from the Campbells and buy a ticket to go back home."

"Aw, Nettie. You won't be any happier there than you are here. Maman worked you like her slave and you know it. At least governesses don't have to do hard work like that. Maybe, the Campbells are nice people and you will enjoy living with them. I'll come see you every Sunday. I'm sure Eugene will, too. Let's stop by his shop. I suspect he's not happy about what papa has done either."

"I don't feel like talking about it right now. Why don't you talk to Eugene after you leave me at the Campbells?" Sarah smiled at her brother. "You know, Fred, when you're not picking on me you are a pretty nice brother. I hope you will visit me…Eugene, too. But I have no intention of visiting with Papa, so don't bring him when you come. You promise?"

"I promise and I don't blame you one bit. He's just an old dirty, slimy, nasty booger." Sarah hid her amusement. Fred still used his favorite childhood expression every chance he got, despite trying to prove how grownup he was.

When they reached the picket fence in front of the recently painted Campbell home, they stood for a moment to study it. On the corner of Bright and Independence Streets, it was one of the nicer houses in the neighborhood and was surrounded by a neatly groomed yard. Camelias banked the house on either side with blossoms in a variety of colors adding cheer to the winter day. Tall pines formed a backdrop for the house. On the left side close to the picket fence, stood a shiny-leaved magnolia. Behind the camelias, four large oaks, now devoid of leaves, would provide shade come summer. Sarah hoped to be gone by then.

"Would you like me to go in with you, Nettie?"

"No, thank you, Fred. You don't need to do that. I'll be fine now."

"Good luck. If you need me…like if they are mean, or terrible or something…just let me know. I'll figure out some way to help you."

Fred was trying hard to look grown up and responsible. Sarah's heart softened with love for her brother. It was good to know that she could count on him and Eugene if things did not go well with the Campbells.

"I know you will, Fred. If they are 'mean, nasty, slimy boogers,' I'll tell you to come rescue me. Now, give me a hug so I can get this over with."

Sarah watched as her brother walked to the corner. When he turned, she waved at him before opening the gate and walking up to the house. Squaring her shoulders, she knocked briskly on the door. She waited so long that she was beginning to turn away when the door opened. The delicious aroma of cinnamon wafted on the air past the plump little woman that stood in the open door. With blue eyes twinkling, she looked Sarah up and down.

"I am sorry I was so slow answering the door. You see, I had to get my apple pies out of the oven before they burned." She paused for a moment before continuing, "My goodness, but aren't you a pretty little thing. Is there something I can do for you, dear?"

Sarah replied, "My father met your husband this morning and

they arranged for me to live here as a tutor for your children."

The woman shook her head, her mouth a perfect O. Immediately Sarah's heart sank. If this woman turned her away, where would she go? The last thing she wanted to do was go back to Nunn's Hotel and plead with her father not to send her away. A series of various future scenarios flickered across her mind. None were appealing.

The woman burst into a wide smile and chuckled. Wiping her hands on her apron, she beckoned Sarah to enter. "You come on in and tell me all about yourself. It's just like dear Mr. Campbell to surprise me this way. He knows I have been fretting about my daughters getting a proper education. I have tried to teach them their letters and a little figuring, but I'm not much good at it, so we had to send them to the public school. Now, when it comes to cooking, I know what I'm doing. You come on back to the kitchen, and we'll have a nice cup of tea and a slice of pie. By the way, I'm Lottie Campbell. What is your name, my dear?"

"I'm Sarah Antoinette Gilbert. My family calls me Nettie, but Sarah is fine."

"Nettie it is. We're going to be good friends, so no need to be formal."

With hope blossoming, Sarah followed the woman down the long central hall and across a covered, brick-floored walkway to a detached kitchen. Looking back at the front door, she wondered how the woman had known she was at the front door. Surely, she could not hear her knock from such a distance.

She had the answer when a small scruffy mutt, yapping madly, ran from the kitchen and sniffed at Sarah's shoes. Bending down, the woman picked up the appealing dog. Sarah could have sworn the animal smiled before Mrs. Campbell put him back on the floor. "Barky announced your arrival, or I would never have known you were out front. I'm sure you can guess why we named him Barky." Lottie chuckled. "Sit down at the table there and I'll pour some tea and dish us up some pie."

"Yes, Madam."

"My word, you sound so elegant. Is that a foreign accent in your voice, Nettie?"

"I grew up speaking French at home. When I speak English, a bit of an accent comes out for certain words."

"French, you say. Are your parents French?"

My father's father, Dr. Ebenezer Gilbert, was from Connecticut. He met my grandmother Elizabeth when she was visiting from Martinique. They fell in love and moved to Martinique to live. That's where my father was born. My mother was a Reynaud from Trinidad. Her parents were French like my grandmother Elizabeth's. My father met my mother, Antoinette, in Trinidad. They were married in 1832 and lived in Trinidad before moving to Middletown, Connecticut, in the late 1830's, where my father has lots of kin. That's where I was born."

"Why, that is just fascinating, Nettie. I do hope you will teach my daughters French."

"Of course, madam."

"None of that 'madam' business, you hear. You call me Miss Lottie."

"Thank you, Miss Lottie." Lottie Campbell put a slice of pie and a cup of tea in front of Sarah. Walking to the opposite side of the table, she placed her own food on the table and seated herself. Picking up her fork, she tasted the pie. "This turned out well. I do hope you will enjoy it."

"It is delicious. I did not eat much lunch, so I am a bit hungry."

Lottie was watching Sarah's face when she said it. Something about her expression told the woman, that the governess thing had come as a shock. Her voice was soft with sympathy when she asked, "So what brings you to Kinston, Nettie? We are not exactly the center of the world." She chuckled as she waited for Sarah's answer.

"My brother Eugene moved here. He has a jewelry shop on Queen Street near the courthouse. My father, my brother Frederick, and I have come to join him."

"Oh yes, I met your brother, Eugene. I had him make me a locket to hold a curl of my sweet little son's hair. My poor baby is with the angels now and this is all I have left of him." Her fingers wandered to the gold locket that hung from a slender chain around her neck. Although her eyes watered, she sniffed back the tears and took a sip of tea.

"I am so sorry. My mother lost babies, too. She still grieves for them."

"It is a sad cross far too many women must bear. I am just grateful I still have my two girls." Lottie added, "Is your mother still living?"

"My mother and my brother Robert are in Hartford where we have been living."

"I look forward to you meeting my girls. They are playing with their friends but should be home soon. Polly is ten, and Jessica is eight. They are well-mannered children, so I don't anticipate any problems for you. Their teacher is not the best and there are too many rowdy boys that she cannot manage. They will be happy to have you teach them. They are just going to love their pretty new governess. Mercy me…'governess'…how grand that sounds. Tell me what you can teach, and I will try to find some books for you. I confess we have few. Do you have musical skills?"

"I sing and play the piano. I am told that I'm good." Sarah added, "I can teach literature, history, geography, dancing, French, and mathematics. I have experience giving music lessons. Do you have a piano?"

"We have a lovely Scherr piano in the parlor. I pretend to play, but I am far from good. My mother played it beautifully. I inherited it from my parents when they passed away. We do have sheet music, but it's not the latest. I will buy some more when we get the books you will need for my girls." Lottie laughed. "My husband will be happy not to listen to me banging on it."

Sarah smiled. Perhaps, being a governess would not be so awful after all. "I look forward to playing it for you and teaching your daughters to play."

"Wonderful." Lottie stood up. "Now that we have finished the pie, let's get you settled. I see you have your valise with you, so I will take you up to the guest room now. I am sorry it has not been aired, but it will only take a few moments to put it to rights. My servant woman, Eliza, is not here presently as I sent her on a shopping errand for some things I need in the kitchen, or I would have her freshen it up. As it is, you and I can get you all settled in two shakes of a lamb's tail."

Sarah started to clear their dishes from the table when Lottie stopped her with a wave of the hand. "Leave it. Eliza will take care of that."

Sarah wanted to ask if Eliza was a slave but decided she

would find out soon enough for herself. She liked Lottie and did not want to think of her as a supporter of slavery.

When Lottie ushered her into the room that was to be hers, Sarah looked around in delight. Sarah noted lace curtains under velvet draperies that would keep out the chill of winter, a fireplace that would soon send warmth into the chilled room, a canopied bed that looked soft and inviting, a large armoire in the corner, and a dressing table with a pitcher and basin on top and a chair beside it. It was the nicest room she had ever had.

"I hope this will be comfortable for you, Nettie. As soon as Eliza returns, I will have her build a fire for you. The chamber pot is under the edge of the bed. She empties it each morning. If there's anything else you need, just let me know. I'm going to leave you now to get settled and put your things away." Noting the small bag Sarah carried, she added, "I see you have few things with you. Do I need my husband to send to the hotel to pick up the rest of your things?"

"Oh, no, thank you. My brother will be shipping my things as soon as I write. Until then, I think I can manage."

"Nonsense. A letter takes too long. Give me your brother's address and I will have Mr. Campbell send a telegram tomorrow."

"Thank you. I confess I would like to have the rest of my clothes, so I don't have to keep wearing the same ones."

"Do you sew?"

"Why, yes, I do."

"I have a bolt of fabric that I don't intend to use. The color is all wrong for me, but it should be lovely on you with that dark hair of yours and those dark blue eyes. I will have Eliza get it out of storage and give it to you. We will simply stitch up a frock for you to have until your other things arrive. We can't have a lovely young woman like you unhappy because she has too few dresses."

Sarah grinned with delight. Lottie did not know it, but for years her dresses had been remade from the castoffs of a wealthy woman to whom she taught piano. She could not remember the last time her parents had given her money to buy a bolt of fabric. "You are too kind, Miss Lottie. Thank you so very much. You make me feel so welcome. I confess, I was worried about coming to live with people I don't know. I feel much better after meeting you. I think I'm going to like it here."

LIFE WITH THE CAMPBELLS
Chapter 3

It was late afternoon when the girls returned. They immediately liked their pretty new governess. While they awaited Mr. Campbell and the evening meal, Sarah played the scales again for Polly who appeared to have inherited her mother's lack of talent, whereas Jessica caught on immediately. Until the ordered schoolbooks arrived, piano and vocal lessons seemed to be the best option. Once Polly could play the scales, Sarah switched to sounding the notes while the two girls tried to mimic the sound. After thirty minutes or so, it was obvious by their fidgeting they were growing tired of the repetition.

"Miss Sarah," Jessica pleaded, "Sing something for us, please."

"I'll just thumb through the music and find a song. First, I will sing it, then we will sing it together."

Sarah gathered the sheet music and thumbed through to find something she thought they might like. Pulling out "Camptown Races," Sarah played it through, singing as she did so. When she finished, she turned to the girls and patted the bench, so they were sitting on either side of her. She pointed to the words of the song. "I'm going to play, and this time I want you to sing with me."

The girls were rendering an enthusiastic "doo dah" when their mother walked into the room and stopped by the door so as not to interrupt. When the final notes died away, Lottie exclaimed, "Sarah, you sing like a bird. Why, you could be another Jenny Lind! Did you know she sang here?"

Sarah looked up in amazement, "In Kinston?"

"Well, no, but nearby. She was on her American tour when her coach broke down about ten miles out of Kinston. The local farm folks gathered around, and she stood under an oak tree and sang for them while the coach was being repaired. Since then, the crossroads is called Jenny Lind in her honor."

"How fortunate they were to hear the most famous singer in the world. I so wish I had been there."

Jenny Lind, The Swedish Nightingale

"As do we all. If the town folks had known, I can tell you there would have been a stampede to get there before she left!" Lottie added, "Since we have our own Jenny Lind now, do you mind if I invite some of my friends to hear you play and sing? It would be such a joy to us all. Would you play another one for me?" Lottie asked.

They all turned at the sound of the front door opening. Michael Campbell hung his coat and hat on the rack by the door and walked toward the sound of music in the parlor. He walked in and stood by Lottie as Sarah was playing and singing the last notes of "Jenny with Her Light Brown Hair."

"You must be Miss Sarah Gilbert. Your father said you could sing and play, but he failed to mention how well. That was beautiful. I pray you will grace our home with your talent often in the coming days."

Turning her head, she met the gaze of the rotund man who was beaming at her. Sarah rose from the Piano bench. Dropping a slight curtsy, Sarah said, "Thank you, sir. It would be my pleasure. Thank you for hiring me as a governess. You have a wonderful family and I look forward to living here with you all."

"You're more than welcome, more than welcome." Michael Campbell patted his wife's shoulder. "I'm about hungry enough to eat a bear."

"Supper is ready, my dear. Shall we go to the dining room?"

Sarah found herself watching the interaction of the family. It was an entirely new experience for her to see the love and kindness they displayed to one another. She could not help the comparison with her own family. What would her childhood have been like, if her mother and father had set the same tone in their household? But then who can look at the past and really know how they would have arrived in the present had things been different. With that thought, her spirits soared. The decision to come to Kinston with her father had quickly gone sour for Sarah prior to meeting the Campbells. What was a callous and selfish act on Joseph Gilbert's part ended up being a blessing for Sarah. Deep in thought, she vaguely registered a question directed her way.

"I'm sorry, Mr. Campbell. I was wool-gathering and did not hear what you said. Please, repeat it and excuse my absent mindedness."

"Of course. I'm sure you are still trying to settle in your mind all the new things that have happened to you in such a short time. What I asked was would you mind playing the piano and singing for us after dinner? Mrs. Campbell, the girls, and I would all so enjoy that. It is our usual habit to read our Bibles following supper while our girls work on their lessons. I think we will all be happy to change our routine this evening.

"Mr. Campbell, yours is the nicest piano I have ever played. It would be a total joy for me to play it any time that you would like. Miss Lottie…Mrs. Campbell…already asked if I would play for some of your friends. I am hoping that soon your daughters will be able to join me in a recital."

Turning to his daughters, Michael Campbell commented, "Girls, I know you are thrilled not to do lessons tonight. I will inform your teacher tomorrow that you will not be returning as you now have private tutelage. In future, Sarah will set your assignments. Tonight, however, we are all having an evening off to enjoy some rare music from our talented Miss Sarah."

After dinner, Sarah sang and played for over an hour for a rapt Campbell audience. Reluctant to end the evening, at last Lottie arose and announced bedtime. Taking candles from a sideboard in the hall, the girls ascended the stairs to their rooms followed by the senior Campbells. With only a candle between them, it was apparent that the girls shared a room. Carrying her own candle, Sarah followed the family up the stairs, turning at the top landing to walk towards the rear of the house and her room. Lottie and Michael Campbell wished her a goodnight as they hugged their daughters and kissed them atop their heads.

With sudden inspiration, Sarah turned back to them and asked, "Would it be permissible to tell Jessica and Polly a bedtime story and tuck them in?"

Neither girl waited for their parent's response, as they chorused, "Please, do!"

Lottie laughed, "You're going to be a treat for these girls of ours. Thank you, Nettie."

Sarah heard Michael ask, as the girl's parents entered their room, "Why do you call her Nettie and not Sarah?" She did not hear the response as their door had closed.

Taking each child by the hand, they walked to the girls' bedroom. Sarah helped them to don their nightgowns, pulled back the covers, and got them settled. Their eyes were bright with anticipation as she began her story, the first of many she would tell in the coming months.

They quickly settled into a routine. In the mornings, the girls worked on their lessons until a late dinner. Afterwards, they practiced at the piano and sang. By three they were restless, so Sarah would send them out to play in nice weather. Since it was a rainy, dreary winter they often decamped to their bedroom to play with their dolls and various toys. From time to time, she would read a fairytale. Each evening, without fail, Michael Campbell would request her to sing and play. Sarah obliged willingly. The only thing that gave her small frissons of warning was the increasingly warm glances he cast her way. Whenever she caught his gaze fixated on her, she was quick to look away.

Fervently, she prayed Miss Lottie was ignorant of those increasingly fond looks. She prayed nothing would happen that would cause her to be cast from a home she had grown to love. Much as a stray and starving animal quickly adopts the house that offers food and affection, Sarah had adopted the Campbells as the family that she wished wholeheartedly were hers. After settling the children in bed, each night she got on her knees by her bed and said her rosary and prayed for guidance.

Sunday afternoons were free time for her. Frequently she would meet her two brothers, and they would stroll about the town. With the coming of Spring, they would sometimes take a picnic that Miss Lottie had Elisa pack for them, and they would sit on the banks of the Cat Hole, a small cove of the muddy Neuse River just off Heritage Street, and enjoy their time together. For her brothers, the treats Elisa included were a reprieve from the boring fare of the Nunn Hotel. Sarah never asked about her father. Frederick occasionally made references to the job at the turpentine factory. She could tell he felt trapped but didn't know how to extricate himself from his father's iron thumb.

Although her family had been raised Catholic and went regularly to their parish church for mass and confessions, Kinston was a Protestant town that afforded no such opportunities for worship. Their Catholic habits quickly slipped from them, and they were satisfied to have these few hours together to enjoy being young with their futures yet unwritten. Sarah still prayed nightly and said the rosary. She doubted that her brothers bothered. Religion for their family had been more habit than heartfelt during their growing up years.

With the coming of summer, the three siblings, accustomed to the cooler winters of New England, were happy to escape to the river where they prayed for an errant breeze to dry perspiration from their brows and provide momentary relief. They found themselves looking forward to the summer storms that rolled in with dark clouds and flashing lightening, accompanied by loud booms of thunder, and torrents of rain. The cool air that followed such storms, would find the three of them on the respective porches at the Nunn Hotel and the Campbell residence breathing in the cooled, ozone-saturated air.

For Sarah, Fall brought not only cooler weather, but her brother Robert. She could not contain her joy as she stood with her brothers and the father she had not seen in months, as they awaited his train. Straining to see down the track, Sarah stood on tiptoe to catch a first glimpse of the scheduled arrival. When her taller brothers obscured the diminutive Sarah's view, she scooted around them and leaned out over the track. She was still ignoring her father. It wasn't until he took her elbow and pulled her back to a safer distance, that she bothered to acknowledge him.

Robert was soon settled into the Nunn Hotel with her brothers. Eugene's business had increased enough that he was able to hire Robert as an apprentice. While it was a job, it did not pay all his expenses. To make ends meet Robert picked up a part-time job at the livery stable on King Street. The owner took a liking to Robert and allowed him to borrow a horse and buggy from time to time. On those occasions, he would take Sarah for a Sunday drive around the outskirts of Kinston.

One Sunday Robert told her that their baby brother, born on the first of June, after Sarah and Fred left Hartford with her father, had been baptized Joseph Ebenezer Gilbert. Sarah stared at him opened mouthed when he told her the baby's name.

"I cannot believe Mother would name him after our father and his father. Does that mean she has forgiven him for leaving?"

"I can't say. All I know is she didn't say anything about wanting to get back with him. I asked her to come with me, but she ignored me." Robert looked away for a moment before adding, "The baby was frail. Sad to say, little Joseph did not survive long after the baptism. Mother was badly grieved by it. God only knows, it seems she mourns the ones she has lost to death far more than the living that left her to move here."

"Cedar Dell" C. 1820,
W. L. Kennedy home, Falling Creek near Kinston

Sarah could not sleep that night for thinking about the brother she had never seen and never would. She arose early and joined Eliza in the kitchen as she prepared breakfast. Elisa soon sat a cup of coffee on the table before her. While Eliza fried the ham and waited for the biscuits to brown, she chatted with Sarah.

Taking the opportunity when no one else was around, Sarah asked, "Are you a slave Eliza? Miss Lottie always calls you her servant, so I wasn't sure."

The woman laughed as she put the last piece of still sizzling ham on the platter. "I be a slave. Quality white folk call us servants. I 'spects it makes 'em feel better."

"Don't you resent it? I would hate to think someone owned me. Most people I know in Connecticut hate the very idea of slavery and want it abolished. Don't you want to be free?"

"Miss Sarah, I got a good life. De Campbells be good folks...kind to me. I been with Miss Lottie since she a baby. She and dem girls be my fambly. I never cared nuthin' 'bout gitting married and havin' babies, so I ain't missin' that. 'Sides, whut I goin' do out der, 'ceptin' starve to death? I gots no skills for nuthin' but cookin' and workin' in de house. I been one lucky darky to git bought for housework and not de fields. Now dat be some hard work. Some of dos field darkies get de whip. I ain't never had to worry none 'bout de Campbells whuppin' me. No siree, I ain't a wantin' to go nowheres but here."

"It just seems so wrong. You could be free and still work for them and get paid."

Eliza shook her head, "Dat's enuff 'bout dis here ole woman. I ain't meanin' no disrespect, but what a pretty little thing like you doin' bein' a servant?"

"When I moved here with my father and brothers, they could not afford to keep me at the hotel with them. My father arranged for me to come here as a governess. This is the first real job I ever had. I helped Mother at home and gave piano and singing lessons sometimes, but that's all. I am grateful that Miss Lottie made me so welcome. I was scared to death when I first came here, thinking I had nowhere to go if she didn't want me."

"Miss Sarah, sump'um fer you to think on." Eliza bent over

to remove the biscuits from the oven before continuing. "I been noticin' how Mr. Campbell lookin' at you and thinkin' on how pretty you be. You gotta be careful. Miss Lottie don't deserve no pussyfootin' around here."

"I know he stares at me too often, Eliza, and I don't know what to do about it. He has never done anything or said anything that was inappropriate. Please know, I would never do anything to hurt Miss Lottie. She has been like a mother to me and far nicer to me than my own."

TROUBLE LOOMS
Chapter 4

By November, it was obvious to Sarah that Robert was unhappy in Kinston. And, more than the other siblings, he felt guilty that they had abandoned their mother. His last letter from her stated that she had moved to New York City just after he had left for Kinston and was working as a seamstress and giving piano lessons. Despite help from his mother's cousin, it was apparent in the letter that her life was far from prosperous. Sarah knew that he was toying with the idea of moving to New York to be with their mother. Another thorn in his side, was the regular criticism he received from Eugene. Robert admitted that he deserved it. He had no talent, no training, and no interest in jewelry or watch making. Sarah begged him not to abandon her. Reluctantly, he promised he would stay until after Christmas. In the meantime, he began to study the employment ads in the American Advocate, Kinston's newspaper. In mid-December, his diligent search appeared to pay off. He was bursting with excitement when he met Sarah the next Sunday afternoon.

"You will never believe what I found," he began. Sarah waited for him to continue. When it was apparent that he was deliberately making her wait, Sarah swatted him on the shoulder.

"Quit teasing me, you big oaf. Tell me!"

"I was looking in the Kinston newspaper and found an ad posted by J. L. Pennington, the newspaper owner in New Berne. He is looking for someone to work in his newspaper. He has another ad looking for a music and singing teacher for the academy there."

"Has he hired you?"

"Not yet. I wrote him a letter telling him of my interest in journalism. I am awaiting his response." With a sheepish look, he added, "I also told him about you."

"Why did you do that? I'm not the one who wants another job." Sarah was upset that he might be leaving her, but more disturbed that he was trying to get her to go as well. Despite Michael Campbell's increasingly amorous glances, she loved living in the Campbell home. It was the first time in her life that she felt adored and valued. Both Polly and Jessica constantly hugged her and told her how much they loved her being their teacher. Under Lottie's unstinting praise and generosity, Sarah felt herself blossoming into someone of worth.

"Don't you see, Nettie, if he hires us both, you can go to New Bern with me."

"Robert, I would sorely hate for you to leave Kinston. Having you nearby means the world to me, but I like the Campbells. I don't know if I would like Mr. Pennington or living in New Berne. Instead of leaving, couldn't you find another job here?"

"I've looked. It's not that I can't find something here, I just don't want to. I've been asking about New Berne. It's located at the junction of the Neuse and Trent Rivers with a bustling port due to its access down the Neuse to the ocean. It's five times the size of Kinston and there's less slavery. I know that slavery bothers you as much as it does me. Plus, New Berne has far more to offer in the way of a city. You don't have to decide until I hear back from Mr. Pennington, but if he wants us, I'm going and I want you to go, too. All I ask is that you think about it."

Sarah was quiet that night at supper and asked the Campbells to excuse her from the habitual singing and playing following dinner. Lottie was immediately alarmed and started clucking over her like a mother hen. Sarah hastened to assure the woman she was not unwell, just suffering from a headache. In less than half an hour, Elisa entered the room bearing a warm cup of willow tea for her pain. Sarah accepted it with gratitude, but the hurt was not in her head. It was in her heart. Once again, her family was going to be fractured. Robert was a gifted writer. If his letter was as well written as she suspected, he probably would get the job. She would be happy for him to do something that had always interested him, but how it would hurt to have him leave her behind.

For days the house had smelled like baking and cooking. Lottie and Elisa were getting ready for the Christmas feast. When she was not with the girls, Sarah joined the two women in the kitchen where she chopped, diced, stirred, and prepped. The smells combined with the easy comradery between them, warmed her heart.

The fruitcakes were in the larder having been made five weeks before Christmas on Stir-up Sunday. Once a week, it was Sarah's job to pour a dram of brandy over each of them. Inside each cake was a good luck coin for the person who got that slice. Lottie explained it would bring good fortune in the coming year to the one who found the coin. Lottie secretly hoped it would be Sarah.

The southern way of celebrating Christmas was all so unlike her childhood memories. Even the dishes were different. Until coming south, Sarah had never had sweet potato souffle, thin cornbread fried crisp in a black skillet in the oven, pecan pies, and a variety of other dishes that utilized local products. Following

New England tradition, Christmases had not been that big a celebration.

The week before Christmas, Lottie shocked her by inviting her brothers and father to join the Campbell family for Christmas dinner at one in the afternoon. She knew the Campbells would attend the nearby Baptist church prior to dinner. As Catholics with no church to attend, the Gilberts would miss services.

Sarah gave her an impulsive hug. "Miss Lottie, that is more than gracious of you. If you don't mind, I will walk to Eugene's store and ask him to tell the others. After eating the hotel food, this is going to be quite a treat for them."

Lottie smiled, "It will be good for you to have your family around you at Christmas. I know we will look forward to meeting Frederick and your father. I have only met Eugene in the shop so I cannot say I know him. For that matter, when Robert arrives to pick you up…despite my invitation…he never comes in. It will be good to get to know him better."

"You must not mind Robert. He is the shyest of us."

"You might want to wash the flour off of your nose before you go to see Eugene." Lottie laughed as Sarah scrubbed her nose until it was red. "Run along now. We will be putting supper on the table when the girls and Mr. Campbell get home."

"I will be back by then. There is no way I want to miss Elisa's fried chicken."

The next few days passed quickly and then it was Monday, Christmas Eve. They all worked that day to decorate the mantle with greenery and put a small tree on a table in the parlor. Sarah and the girls had made paper decorations for the tree, strung popcorn, and tied on colorful ribbons. The girls were beyond excited by the results of their hours of work.

Sarah had spent days in her room making gifts for the Campbell family while the girls were out playing with their friends. She was looking forward to gathering in the parlor after dinner and presenting them. For Michael Campbell she had embroidered his initials and family crest on a fine cotton handkerchief. Lottie's gift was a shawl she had made from a length of leftover silk and decorated with embroidered flowers that had taken her hours to stitch. Sarah was proud of it. For the girls, she had used scrap fabric from their Sunday dresses to make matching outfits for their dolls. The only other gift was one for Robert. She had found a desk set in one of the small shops on Queen Street. Covered in dust and shoved in a back corner, she was able to buy it for a modest price out of money she had saved from her salary. It sat in the corner of her room, newly cleaned and shiny. She planned to give it to him after Christmas dinner.

On Christmas Eve, Sarah joined the Campbells in the parlor. She seated herself at the piano and began playing Christmas carols. This time the family joined her in singing the accustomed songs. When it was time to open the presents, Sarah handed the Campbells the ones she had made for them. Judging by their faces and exclamations of delight, she had chosen well. When it was her turn to open her gift, she gasped in delight. Inside the wrappings was a neatly folded ballgown with matching slippers, a fan, and a thin gold bracelet.

Lottie watched Sarah's face suffuse with joy. "I am so glad you like them, Nettie. You are young and beautiful. Before too long, some young man is going to be squiring you around. We must see you get out more, so you have a chance to socialize. Perhaps after Christmas, we will have the soiree I mentioned when you first came. I want our friends to see our accomplished young governess. Many of them have sons your age that you should meet."

Sarah looked down and blushed. Michael had looked uncomfortable when Lottie mentioned her meeting young men. She wished he would not stare at her so intently, making her uneasy and constantly wary. Pushing the thought aside, she joined Polly and Jessica as they admired their gifts.

Christmas dawned clear and cold. Eugene had passed the dinner invitation to his brothers and father and they sent a note of acceptance. At the appointed hour, the four men knocked on the door of the Campbell's house. Except for Robert who had a small package for Sarah in his coat pocket, they arrived with no gifts. Sarah hurried to answer the door and let them in. In the foyer, they hung their hats and coats on the hat rack before following her to the parlor where she introduced them to the waiting Campbell family. After a few minutes of polite chatter, Lottie invited them into the dining room where the sideboard was weighed down with the bountiful feast Sarah had helped prepare. After months of avoiding her father, she was nervous being around him. He appeared none too comfortable either. Other than a curt greeting, she ignored him during the meal and was grateful that Lottie had seated him at the opposite end of the table next to Mr. Campbell.

It was during dessert that Robert cleared his throat to speak. "First, I want to thank you Mr. and Mrs. Campbell for inviting us to eat Christmas dinner with you. I think it just may be the best meal I ever had. It was most kind of you to include us in your family celebration. I can see why Sarah thinks so highly of you. I..."

Interrupting Robert, Joseph Gilbert could not avoid the boast,

"I always try to look out for my children. I knew this would be good for Nettie the minute I met Mr. Campbell here. I hope Nettie is sufficiently grateful to you for taking her in."

Lottie looked from Sarah's bent head to her gloating father. She did not like the man; but hid the rancor behind a polite smile. "It is we who are grateful, Mr. Gilbert. Sarah has been a wonderful addition to our home. She has become like another daughter to me. Not only has she worked to educate our daughters, she also has helped me with cooking and other chores and has been gracious enough to entertain us with her singing and playing."

Determined to finish what he wanted to say, Robert cut his father off when he saw him open his mouth to comment. "As I was about to say, I want to take this occasion to make an announcement. Yesterday I received a response to a letter I wrote a Mr. Pennington in New Berne. He has offered me a job as a reporter for his newspaper. I will be moving to New Berne."

Lottie looked at the members of the Gilbert family. The two brothers and father looked shocked. Joseph Gilbert's face was slowly turning red with suppressed anger. She read sadness in Sarah's face, but no surprise at the news. She could only surmise that Sarah was aware of what Robert was planning. Knowing how close the two were, this would be a blow to her.

Joseph stood, with a cold voice and set face, he said, "On behalf of my family, I want to add my appreciate for this fine meal. We would linger, but it seems we have some things to discuss. Boys, make your goodbyes."

Robert shook his head in defiance of the order, "I will be a few minutes more, Papa. I need to talk to Sarah in private. Mrs. Campbell, Mr. Campbell, will you excuse us, please."

Lottie motioned to the parlor, "You two go on in there where it's warm. I think I saw something under the tree with your name on it, Robert. Mr. Campbell and my daughters will linger here for a bit to let our dinner settle."

Without another word, Joseph Gilbert motioned to Frederick and Eugene to follow him out. When they had left, Robert and Sarah arose from the table and went to the parlor. Sarah could not prevent the slow seep of tears from her eyes as she followed Robert in. Walking to the fireplace, she stretched her hands to the warmth, her back to her brother.

"Don't be sad, Sarah," Robert began. "Let me give you my gift and then I want to tell you my other surprise."

Turning from the fire, Sarah announced, "I have something for you, too. However, I'm not sure I want any more surprises."

While she recovered her gift for him from under the tree, he stepped into the hall and fished the one he had for her from his coat. Walking back into the parlor, he thrust the small package into her hands. Taking it, Sarah removed the wrapping paper and peered into the small box it had contained. There on a soft silk pad was a beautiful gold locket.

"I made it for you. It's not as well-crafted as Eugene can make, but I want you to have it."

"It's beautiful, Robert. It may be the nicest gift I ever got, and knowing how much you dislike jewelry making, it makes it even more precious that you would do this for me."

"You deserve it, Nettie." Robert looked at the large package she had set on the table by the tree. "Is that for me?"

Sarah beamed, "It is. I hope you will like it."

Robert was delighted with his gift and exclaimed over the pen, paper, and small writing chest. It seemed an omen for his future as a journalist. "This reminds me, Sarah. Mr. Pennington is also offering you a position at the academy. He says you may stay with him and his wife, as they have a couple of extra rooms. I will stay there, as well, and share a room with a printer's apprentice. He said the rent will be modest and he will deduct it from our salaries. He sent me two train tickets, too."

"Robert, I told you that I'm happy here. I'm not miserable like you are. I don't want you to leave, but I don't see how I can go with you after the Campbells have been so good to me."

"You have a few days to think about it. Don't say 'no' too fast." Robert grimaced, "I suppose I should get back to the hotel and prepare to get my ears blistered. Eugene is going to be alright about me leaving because he was not too thrilled with my work. But you know how Papa is. If he's not in charge of things, he gets angry. At twenty-four, I'm a grown man. Eugene is twenty-five, for goodness sake. I don't know how Eugene takes his bossing. I, for one, am tired of it. It's time I got out from under his thumb."

SARAH GOES TO NEW BERNE
Chapter 5

Sarah shifted on the wooden bench, her reticule on her lap. She bit her lip as she watched the streets of Kinston slip past the train window to be replaced by small isolated farms and endless stretches of pines that were occasionally interrupted by small pocosins, their water black in the overcast day. From time to time, a silent tear would trickle from her eyes and roll down her cheeks where they hung until they dropped onto her pelisse. Robert, on the bench beside her, glanced uneasily in her direction. He could not avoid the shock he felt when Sarah appeared at the station with her luggage. He had thought she would come merely to see him off. Just two days previous, she had vehemently rejected his pleas to move to New Berne with him. It was a good thing, he thought, that he had not written Pennington that Sarah did not want the job.

After miles of silence and repeated rebuffs of any conversation he tried to start, he finally blurted, "Nettie, what happened to make you change your mind? Whatever it was, you don't look very happy to be going to New Berne."

"I can't talk about it, Robert. Please don't ask. I just decided this is for the best."

"I want you to be happy, too. I'm so looking forward to joining the paper and doing something I'm good at. It will ruin it for me if you are miserable."

"It is difficult when I know little of where we are going except what I've been told. And, what's worse, I know nothing of the

Penningtons beyond the fact that he hired you for his newspaper and me to teach French in the Academy."

"You didn't know what the Campbells would be like either. Yet, you ended up loving them. Just give the Penningtons a chance. Mr. Pennington seemed really gracious in his letter."

Sarah did not reply, just resumed looking out the window. How could she tell her brother why she was leaving? How could she tell him that Michael Campbell had entered her room the night before last? She had awakened to find him leaning over her. Sarah shuddered when she remembered how she had slapped him…hissing at him to get out of her room before she started screaming. He had begged her not to tell Lottie. He did not need to ask. She could not bear to think of hurting Lottie by telling her what her husband had done. It gave Sarah no choice but to leave. Lottie, Jessica, and Polly were all in the kitchen the next morning making gingerbread cookies when Sarah told them she was going with her brother to New Berne. The three of them cried and pleaded with her to change her mind. Despite tears in her own eyes, Sarah was adamant.

Eliza caught her eye, giving a quick jerk of her chin. She suspected the reason for Sarah's decision to leave. "Now, y'all don't go plaguin' Miz Sarah. She doin' whut's bes' fer her. We been lucky fer havin' her dis long."

"Oh, I know, Eliza," Lottie cried. "It's just that Nettie has become like a daughter to me and my girls love her so. And, just think of the joy Mr. Campbell has had listening to her sing and play."

"Yes'em, I seen how he like it," her voice was flat when she said it. "Still, dis gwine be fer de better fer Miz Sarah."

Lottie told her husband that night at the dinner table. His

quiet comment was that it was probably for the best. Lottie looked at him in puzzlement that he was taking it so well when he so enjoyed Sarah's musical evenings. Trying to hide how flustered he was, Michael Campbell expounded on how much New Berne had to offer compared to a much smaller town like Kinston. Sarah excused herself from the table while he was talking and went to her room to pack. There would be no playing and singing for them her last night. She was in bed when someone knocked on her door.

She struggled to hide the momentary panic in her voice, by asking who was there. Lottie replied that she wanted to come in for a moment as Sarah would be leaving early in the morning with little time for goodbyes. Lottie entered the room and sat on the foot of Sarah's bed.

Lottie's eyes were shiny with tears, when she said, "Nettie, if things don't work out in New Berne, you know you are always welcome here."

"Thank you. I want you to know how much I appreciate all you have done for me. I love you like a mother, and I will never forget you. I promise to write to you when I get settled in New Berne."

"I would like that, Nettie. I asked Eliza to have a package of food for you to take on the train, so stop by the kitchen before you leave in the morning." Reaching in her pocket, she pulled out a small box and an envelope. "These pearls belonged to my mother. I want you to have them. The envelope is a little something extra to help you buy whatever you might need to get settled in a new place."

Sarah gasped, "You have already paid me. This is too much. The pearls should go to one of your daughters."

"You *are* one of my daughters, Nettie." At that, both women began to cry. Lottie wrapped her in her arms and whispered, "Go with God, Nettie. Remember, I'm always here for you."

Sitting on the train the next day, the scene kept playing in her mind. The secret of Lottie Campbell's betrayal by her husband would go with Sarah to her grave. She was good at keeping secrets. She had no way of foreseeing how important that skill would be in her future.

Sarah felt the train slowing as they reached New Berne. When the whistle blew to announce their arrival, despite herself, she felt an upwelling of exhilaration. The town was pretty, sitting on a bluff of the Neuse River with pine and magnolia trees turning the winter-scape green. Standing at the depot, stood a tall, conservatively dressed man of no more than early thirties. Behind him stood a negro servant. When Sarah and Robert stepped off the train, the man immediately hailed them, sending the servant to collect their valises.

Sarah studied John Pennington as he introduced himself. The man oozed dignity and seriousness. There was an intensity about him evident in the very tilt of his shoulders and the timbre of his voice. This was not a man with time to trifle with her. He was all business. If he noticed her looks, he gave no indication after the brief introductions.

For a moment she was a tiny bit peeved. She was accustomed to drawing admiring glances from men. Despite her lack of stature, she was possessed of a high full bust, tiny waist, and rounded hips. Her classic features were accented by an abundance of curling dark hair and sparkling blue eyes fringed with long dark lashes. On reflection, she decided it was a very good thing that he ignored her looks.

He was far more interested in Robert, explaining that the times were momentous, and he would need help to adequately cover the politics of the day in his paper. Sarah wondered if Robert were as ignorant of what was happening in the country as she. At the Campbells, there had never been any attention paid to politics. If Mr. Campbell had any interest in national affairs, he did not express them in his home. Lottie was happily oblivious to anything beyond her front door. Thus, Sarah had gone from one pleasant day to the next untroubled by the outside world...the only annoyance: Michael Campbell's ogling. She suspected that was the last thing to worry about from John Pennington.

When they reached his two story, Georgian style house with neatly groomed yard, Sarah admired the dark shutters against light brick walls, a pristine brick walk leading to a fan-lighted front door, and clean glass sparkling in the milky midday sun that was bravely trying to cancel gray skies. He opened the door and motioned for Sarah and then Robert to enter. When they walked into the elegant foyer, the siblings admired the polished walnut and mahogany furnishings and noted with pleasure that the house boasted of gas lights. A stately and comely young woman came down the hall to greet them. He introduced her as his wife Kate. His voice caressed the name. He added that they had a two-year old daughter named Kate, as well, but they called her Katie. His wife invited them to come to the dining room for the waiting dinner. As she turned to lead them, Sarah spied a child, that had been hidden from view, clinging to her mother's skirts with her right hand, the left thumb firmly stuck in her mouth. John Pennington's laughter lightened his countenance as he leaned down and swooped his daughter into his left arm. His right hand rested on his wife's waist. It was obvious the man was besotted by his family. Sarah did not realize she had exhaled in relief until she caught Robert looking at her with a puzzled expression in his eyes. Her answer was a wide smile. She would not need to worry about John Pennington becoming enamored of her.

After that, Sarah was able to relax and follow the conversation between Robert and Mr. Pennington. He was furious that the Democrats had nominated Buchannan, rather than Douglas, thus assuring a loss to the Illinois lawyer, Abraham Lincoln, in the November Presidential election.

"It may well mean war, mark my words. It's a sad prospect, indeed, as I had hoped we could hold this Union together. However, as I wrote in my paper, The Daily Progress, 'if our northern neighbors insist upon regarding slaves in the south as a moral taint which it is their duty to eradicate, we must quit them'."

From the opposite end of the table, Kate chuckled, "Must we be so serious dear. I would like to hear a little about our lovely new guest and her brother. You will have all the time you need later to fill Robert in about what's going on here and elsewhere."

At Kate's prompting, Sarah explained her family heritage and that they had come to Kinston the previous January to join her brother Eugene who was working as a jeweler. She described working as a governess in Kinston and her teaching duties.

Robert interrupted, "What Sarah isn't telling you is that she is a very gifted musician, both on the piano and vocally."

"Why that's wonderful. Both Mr. Pennington and I are ardent supporters of the arts in New Berne. I do hope you will share your gifts with us."

"It would be my pleasure."

Mr. Pennington inserted, "We have a theater, Lowthorpe Hall, where traveling troops perform, as well as talented locals. No doubt, you will find that of interest, and they will be delighted to have you. There are frequent dances at the Gaston House Hotel on Friday nights. The dances are popular with young and old alike.

Gaston House Hotel

We also have a local dance academy led by a fine young man from Rowan County by the name of Rowan Slater. There is an excellent bookstore owned by F. W. Beers where you can buy northern newspapers, various stationery supplies, and the latest books. On Middle Street there's a soda shop which is popular for its ice cream come summer. Then there's the Academy. I'm proud to say the New Berne Academy is the first public school in North Carolina. We have several banks, a Masonic Lodge, and a variety of shops. The river and local farms supply us well with a plethora of seafood, vegetables, eggs, and meats. What is not available locally is easily imported through our fine port. The LaRoque shipping firm brings our ladies goods from as far away as Europe. They also bring in molasses, pineapple, and various products from the Caribbean. You will discover New Berne is a vibrant town. Some call it the *Athens of the South*. I suspect you two will enjoy it here. Also, it's not so far that you cannot take the train to Kinston to visit the others of your family from time to time."

When dinner was done, Kate arose saying, "Sarah, Robert, I will show you to your rooms so you can get settled. Mr. Pennington will walk you to his office in the morning, get Robert settled and then walk you, Sarah, to the Academy and introduce you to the Headmaster. Today, I thought it would be nice, once you're settled, if you used the afternoon to acquaint yourself with our town. We have supper at 5:30. That should give you time enough for a little tour."

When they had finished unpacking in their assigned rooms, Robert rapped on Sarah's door. She joined him in the hall, and they left to walk to the water and business district. Some of her misgivings eased as she walked along the board sidewalks towards the port admiring the shops along the way. The port was crowded with ships off-loading wares. Hogsheads of tobacco and bales of cotton waited quayside for loading. At the end of the row of wharfs, they spied the LaRoque shipping company that Mr. Pennington had mentioned. Beyond the ships, the water stretched over a mile wide at the junction of the Neuse and Trent Rivers. Later they learned where the rivers joined was called Union Point. When they turned to walk back, a beautiful young woman, with blond hair and wearing the latest of styles, emerged from the LaRoque office. Sarah caught Robert turning for a second look.

Union Point, New Berne

"I guess you think New Berne gets better looking all the time?"

"If all the girls are as pretty as that one, I'm going to like it here just fine." Robert grinned, "I've seen some men give you the once-over, too. Don't try to pretend you didn't notice, because I saw you preening."

Sarah swatted his sleeve. "Don't tease me and I won't tease you."

"You started it." Robert laughed and took her elbow to guide her across the street to see the shops on the opposite side.

Middle Street, New Berne

They were back at the Pennington house on Pollock Street by the appointed hour. As Mr. Pennington was late returning home, Kate showed Sarah the piano in the parlor and their collection of sheet music. Robert loved music too and joined his sister at the piano. His baritone was not as fine a voice as Sarah's, but they harmonized well together. He thumbed through the music while Sarah tested the tone of the Piano.

After supper, Sarah asked the Penningtons if she and Robert could provide a little entertainment. They both beamed with pleasure. While the parents went through the goodnight ritual with Katie, Sarah and Robert sorted through the collection of sheet music for the pieces they would perform. The Penningtons joined Sarah and Robert in the parlor once Katie was settled in bed.

After an hour, Mr. Pennington clapped with vigorous appreciation and was quickly joined by Kate in acknowledging the two Gilberts. He exclaimed, "We had no idea you two were so gifted. I can't say when I've enjoyed an evening of music more. You must allow us to invite some of our friends over for a soiree one evening soon. For now, I suspect it's bedtime. I'll see you in the morning. We have breakfast at 6:30. You will need to be ready to leave by seven."

A MATCH NOT MADE IN HEAVEN
Chapter 6

The New Berne Academy was a handsome two-story brick, cupola-crowned building on the corner of Middle and New Streets. Just as Pennington boasted to Robert that New Berne had the first printing press and the first newspaper in North Carolina, he reminded Sarah that the Academy was the oldest public school in North Carolina, having been erected first in 1764 and following a fire, rebuilt in 1810. It was supported by a tax on liquor and included students of both sexes who paid a fee to attend. It also admitted a few indigent pupils at no charge. Sarah was introduced to the headmaster, Dr. William Barton, and the teachers, Miss Hancock and Miss Brent. With the introductions done, Pennington left. Miss Barton led her to the second-floor classroom that she would use to teach French and literature. Music would be on the lower level where the required piano was located. She would be teaching one class a day in French, one in music, and two in reading the classics. When she learned of the last class, she quailed. Of all the classes to be delegated to her, that was not one she expected. When Robert answered the ad, it had not mentioned anything except an instructor for French. The music was a surprise but represented no challenge. That she had taught before. It was the literature. Despite having been an outstanding student when she was in school, she was not ready for that. She could foresee many nights of reading by candlelight…and little sleep…in order to stay ahead of her students and prepare the next day's instruction.

New Berne Academy

Her teaching salary was enough to afford room and board with the Penningtons and still provide enough for her necessities and a few luxuries. The gold coins Lottie had given her she would save for some unforeseeable necessity. She sewed them carefully into the lining of her pelisse for safekeeping, and there they would stay...her emergency escape hatch.

While Lottie was warm and motherly, Kate Pennington soon became Sarah's first real girlfriend. In opposition to her husband, the woman was light-hearted, impulsive, and given to gales of laughter. Sarah was amused and a little embarrassed when Kate told her she was sadly lacking in the skills of flirtation. She did not want to tell the woman that her parents had given her no opportunity to use feminine allure by restricting any exposure to young single men.   Undaunted by Sarah's self-conscious reluctance, Kate unfurled her fan, batted eyelashes, gave a flirtatious look, and a come-hither smile to demonstrate a few feminine wiles. Soon both women were laughing until tears rolled down their cheeks. While she did not have a mother figure in Kate, she had a youthful woman that made her laugh. A bonus was the fact that John Pennington was so besotted of his wife, he never gave Sarah more than a friendly nod and smile...no amorous looks. His conversations at dinner were mainly confined to ongoing angst over the political situation that he shared ad nauseum with Robert who seemed to relish it. She and Kate held separate conversations at the opposite end of the dining table.

Pollock Street, New Berne

Despite her initial trepidation, New Berne was proving to be far more pleasant than she anticipated. She loved to walk down to Union Point and stare across the broad water to the green, pine-studded distant bank. On the city side of the river, feathery-leaved trees growing along the edge of the river pushed up knobby roots. She learned these trees were called cypress. Coming from New England, she was charmed by the novelty of them.

Two weeks after her arrival in New Berne, John Pennington announced that he had invited Rowan Slater for Saturday dinner. Pennington gave Kate a significant look when he announced the invitation. Sarah suspected Kate had put him up to it. Days earlier, Kate had been none too subtle when she extolled the man's attributes. Rowan, from a prominent family just outside Salisbury, was a graduate of Trinity College. He had his own dance academy where he also gave instruction in music. He was a proficient violinist and according to Kate, a perfect catch.

At the dinner, Kate placed Sarah and Rowan side by side at the table. Sarah was flustered when she found Kate and John watching her and Rowan. Taking a deep breath, she decided to ignore them. Rowan was an adept conversationalist and soon had her responding with ease to his questions. John had told Rowan that she was teaching music at the Academy, as well as French and literature. With that advanced information in mind, he invited her to join him in the parlor for an impromptu musical performance. Sarah was nervous at the idea. She was naturally gifted, but her only formal musical instruction was from her mother. She did not know if she could meet the expectations of someone college educated. The Penningtons, abetted by Robert, gave her no quarter as they insisted on Sarah playing the piano and singing while he accompanied her on the violin.

To her surprise, he was more than laudatory about her skill. Sarah glowed with the accolade. A tiny flicker of interest in the man, quickly flared into a desire to see more of him. She did not realize it, but Rowan Slater was smitten from his first glimpse of the beauteous Sarah. Soon, Sarah and Rowan were an item. He called on her every Sunday afternoon, and they walked along the streets of New Berne, invariably ending at Union Point. Sarah became a frequent partner at the Friday night balls that he hosted at the Gaston House Hotel. Although Sarah was untutored in dancing, under his instruction and with her natural sense of rhythm, they were soon gliding around the dance floor. Wearing the ball gown and bracelet and pearls given her by the Campbells, Sarah found herself preening at the attention she garnered from available men. While she found the admiration welcome, Rowan Slater gave her no opportunity to act on the invitations that came her way from other would-be swains.

As winter evolved into an early March spring, forsythia, redbud, cherry, daffodil, and jasmine joined tender green leaves as they emerged into the warming air. Soon New Berne awakened to the verdant joy of the changed season. With an ominous cloud on the horizon, the tranquil days of spring would not last.

On Sunday, April 14, 1861, John Pennington came home at ten in the morning frothing with fury. Along with Robert and many other citizens of the town, he had stood in the depot when a special train arrived from New Berne announcing the fall of Fort Sumter. When Lincoln refused to turn the federal fort over to the state, hot heads in South Carolina had fired on Fort Sumter in Charleston harbor for two days leading to its surrender on April 13. He railed throughout the noon meal that the war he had feared, and the dissolution of the Union, were both inevitable. With support growing for severing the Union, two months earlier Craven County had approved by a margin of over five hundred votes a resolution to secede should South Carolina do so. As soon as they could bolt down their dinner, Robert and he rushed back to the newspaper to read the telegrams that came pouring in by the minute. Kate and Sarah sat on at the table.

While Kate patiently encouraged Katie to eat her food, she mourned what the events in South Carolina would mean for her husband. "Oh, dear God, Sarah. As much as he hates the thought of war and the breaking up of the Union, I fear he will think it his duty to join the local militia should it come to that. His health is not such as that needed for warfare in various seasons. He is much too prone to catarrh."

Sarah thought of her brothers and Rowan. Would they feel the need to take up arms? As a North Carolinian by birth and despite his somewhat effete interests, Rowan might well feel pressure to enlist. Her brothers detested slavery. Their roots were in the North. If they were to march to war, on which side would they fight? Sarah felt the security she had begun to feel in New Berne was collapsing as rapidly as the Union.

As for John Pennington, he was too busy to worry about his lungs. In a special edition, he declared in sudden *volta-face*: 'The south is now our country and our country demands our allegiance; our section, our honor, our interests and all that we hold dear upon earth calls us to arms! Are there any whose craven hearts will shrink from a duty so palpable?' When a special train arrived on Monday bringing word that Lincoln was demanding troops, Pennington's newspaper declared 'a war of coercion has been openly proclaimed.' He added, 'If divisions existed before upon the true policy of the country, the proclamation of Lincoln has served to disperse them and make our people unite.'

That night, the New Berne militia company started on a self-proclaimed mission to free Fort Macon...some twenty-five miles distant on the outer banks...from Union occupation. Situated at the terminus of the Neuse river and on the inlet at Beaufort, the fort was vital to keeping New Berne's port open in the event of war.

Fort Macon, Bogue Banks, N.C.

Much to the elation of New Berne, Fort Macon soon fell to the ill-equipped and poorly trained rebels. That was no great feat as the fort was poorly defended by only a small force of Union soldiers.

It was not until a letter arrived two weeks later, that Sarah learned Eugene had joined the Goldsborough Volunteers that was being assigned to occupy Fort Macon. With Eugene fighting in the Confederate forces, on May 29, Robert enlisted in Company 1 of the 2nd North Carolina Infantry. Suddenly her world was upside down.   John Pennington was anticipating closing the newspaper and joining the military. The Academy was closing leaving her with no employment.

Saddened by the prospect of leaving Rowan and the delightful balls, and in an agony of worry for her brothers, Sarah felt she had no choice but to obey a peremptory summons from her father, bid Rowan and the Penningtons farewell, and join her father and Frederick in Goldsborough. Rowan walked her to the station where he asked her to wait for him, declaring his love for her. She smiled without answering. He stood forlorn, hat in hand, as she climbed on the train to Goldsborough and waved goodbye.

Refusing to allow the woman he loved to remove herself from him, a determined Rowan soon followed her to Goldsborough. On June 12, 1861, with Frederick and Joseph Gilbert as witnesses, Sarah and Rowan said their vows in front of Reverend W. C. Hunter in St. Stephen's Episcopal Church. She was eighteen and her groom twenty-six. They were just one couple among many who married in the excitement of war.

Rowan found employment as a purchasing agent for the Confederate Government while Sarah struggled to settle into domestic life. The chores that she had hated when helping her mother in their boarding house were again her daily lot as she kept house for her husband, father, and brother. For Sarah, without the dancing and gaiety of life in New Berne during their courting days, the thrill of wedded life was wearing a bit thin.

In December of 1862, General John G. Foster leading Union troops from occupied New Bern, fought a fierce battle at the railroad bridge over the Neuse River near Goldsborough in an effort to destroy the line that carried war matériel from the port in Wilmington to Confederate warehouses in Richmond. The bridge was damaged, but soon repaired and rail service resumed. In January of 1863, Eugene returned to Goldsborough as a guard on the Wilmington and Weldon Railroad as the town was a convenient base. He was shortly enlisted to help Sarah care for the morbidly ill Fred who had enlisted in the infantry in March of 1863. Like many in the Confederate army, he was soon ill with measles. Then it was…one brother ill, another brother, a father, and a husband in the house…all for whom she must care and cook. An added nettle was the deep rancor that Sarah still felt for Joseph since he had thrown her out of the Kinston hotel the day after they arrived. Despite her diligent care, on June 8, Frederick Gilbert, aged seventeen, was laid to rest in the Goldsborough Cemetery. Still grieving for her youngest brother, Sarah reached the end of her rope when Rowan was assigned to a position in Charleston.

With Rowan in Charleston, Frederick dead, and Eugene frequently away, Sarah spent her time avoiding her father as much as possible and moping. It was not until July of 1863, that the newly-weds were reunited. He had written her that he was on furlough to recover from a debilitating bout with Yellow Fever and would be traveling to his family home outside Salisbury. In his letter Rowan enclosed the money she would need for rail tickets to join him. Sarah was glad to leave Goldsborough and her father behind despite not knowing what to expect in the new location.

Once more on a train to a new home, Sarah had time to question if hers was a genuine love for her husband. She had never had the opportunity to be courted by others and thus had no one with whom to compare Rowan. In the cold light of day,

Sarah suspected her marriage was a mistake. As a dance partner, Rowan had excited her, but there was no dancing in the middle of war. Furthermore, Sarah wanted more in her life than endless years of drudgery keeping house for a husband from whom she felt increasingly estranged. Furthermore, she had no desire to be tied down by the inevitable children.

It was an exhausting trek from Goldsboro to Raleigh, Kinston to Goldsborough, and then on to Raleigh where she would change to the Western Carolina Railroad that would take her past Hillsborough, Company Shops, Greensborough, and Lexington before the final stop in Salisbury. Bedraggled and out of sorts, she stepped from the train in Salisbury to an enthusiastic welcome from her husband who still sported a sallow complexion from his recent illness. She tried to return the ardor of his welcome, but her heart was not in it. Had it ever been?

An embarrassed Rowan informed Sarah of his family and the intricacies that had resulted from his father's precipitous death in 1836 leaving his wife with five children, the youngest Rowan. Three years after her husband's death, the widow married her plantation overseer, Remus West. It was not a happy household. To relieve marital pressure on their mother, his sister Mary moved Rowan, then six years of age, in with her and her husband, William Overman, a wagon maker. His brother James was taken in by his sister Jane who was married to the prosperous Salisbury merchant, John D. Brown. When they came of age, the two musically gifted brothers were sent to Trinity College in nearby Randolph county. Rowan explained that they would be moving in with his mother on the family farm. He did not tell her how reluctant his mother was to have them.

The city-raised Sarah had no clue what living on a farm would entail. She soon learned. With their slaves gone, family members were expected to work in the fields and gardens. While she found household work drudgery, she soon learned that farm work was far more onerous in the hot Carolina summer. Even worse was the lack of respect given to the couple by Rowan's mother and her husband. While Rowan was viewed as an ineffectual do-nothing with pretentions of grandeur, she was a Yankee outsider in a land that despised northerners. She felt that every morsel she ate, despite how hard she worked to harvest and prepare it, was begrudged by the parsimonious Remus West. Her mother-in-law was little more welcoming. Sarah suspected that the death of her prominent first husband and remarriage to a lower-class overseer had left her embittered and angry at fate.

Adding to her misery at enforced cohabitation on a farm with people she did not even like…and that equally disliked her…was the nearby prison. Sarah came to despise Salisbury with its odorous prison for Yankee captives…men who were starving, poorly housed, disease ridden, and in circumstances lower than the poorest of poor. She wondered if any of the skeletal men behind the prison fences were men that she had known, perhaps gone to school with, in Middletown or Hartford. Food was short for everyone, but for the hapless prisoners there was barely enough to sustain life. Nor were there medicines to treat diarrhea and the diseases that plagued them. Further exacerbating conditions, the prison became increasingly crowded when Richmond started sending prisoners from the prison there to Salisbury so they would be further from Union lines should they try to escape. Her heart ached whenever she passed the dismal compound. an abandoned textile mill that was ill-suited for the purpose of housing so many men. Even worse were the trenches of mass graves in a nearby cotton field, a grim reminder that for twenty-six percent of prisoners in Salisbury the only exit was death.

Salisbury Prison, Rowan Co., N.C.

Soon she had even more reason to despise prisons. On November 29, 1863, Eugene was arrested for encouraging desertion from the Confederate army and imprisoned. Robert, who was there at the time, wrote Sarah to tell her about the trial. When General Robert E. Lee granted the appeal for clemency, in December, Robert...despite a fine war record...joined Eugene and they fled from the Wise Forks encampment near Kinston. Robert wrote Sarah that they were headed for New Bern. Her two brothers were now shadow-people of an unknown location, one that would remain a mystery through all the years to come. There would never be any documentation to show if they had reached New Bern.

She could not decide if she was relieved or terrified when Rowan re-enlisted on July 23, 1864. She considered it a stroke of luck that he was leaving without getting her pregnant. She was weary of him and weary of life with his family, but he had proven a buffer of sorts between her and the constant harping from his mother and stepfather about the Yankee in their midst and the burden of two extra mouths to feed.   Following Rowan's departure, she endured as best she could.

Plowing the fields

For the rest of the unbearably hot summer, Sarah gathered produce from the garden and helped her mother-in-law with preserving the food for winter. Then came autumn and the next round of harvesting late ripening crops. The cooler weather was a relief, but the change in temperature did nothing to ease the sore muscles in her back and shoulders. The slaughter of hogs to make bacon, ham, sausage, lard and a variety of porcine products arrived with the cold of winter. The entire process sickened her. She forced herself to swallow the bile that arose in her throat and doggedly do what they told her. But, no matter had hard she tried, it was never going to be quite good enough.

It would have been better if she had managed to establish some rapport with Alice Slater West. It was obvious early on that would not happen. Neither Alice nor her husband hid their disdain for her French-tinged northern accent. Sarah's comments about Rowan were met with a snide remark. They only halfway listened when she read them passages from Rowan's letters. It didn't take long to deduce that they considered her husband the black sheep of the family.

After a particularly difficult day, Sarah had had enough of the constant needling. She went to her room late that afternoon and ripped the emergency gold coins Lottie had given her out of her pelisse lining and packed her bags. Sarah left the following morning without a word to her in-laws. Living in New York with her mother could not be as bad as living in Salisbury with Rowan's mother and stepfather.

Furthermore, unlike North Carolina, the soil of the North had not been ravaged by a war that brought extreme deprivation of the many things needed for daily life. She was tired of ersatz coffee sweetened with honey when they could find it. Tired of the endless pork, cornbread, and sweet potatoes. Tired of old clothes, worn out shoes, buttons and hair pins carved from wood, and a myriad of other small inconveniences that caused daily annoyance in the war-torn South. It was time to seize her fate and make it one that brought her the things she wanted in life.

SECRETARY SEDDON FINDS A FRESH FACE
Chapter 7

Sarah walked up to the ticket window to purchase her ticket. "I would like a ticket to New York City, please. One way only."

"Little lady, with a war on you can't just buy a ticket to anywhere north of the Mason-Dixon Line. You must obtain permission to travel to New York. I can sell you a ticket to Richmond, then you have to get a permit to travel north."

"But, where do I go and whom must I see for permission?"

"I suspect the best thing would be for you to go to our two North Carolina congressmen, James Ramsey and Burgess Gaither. If they both agree to give you a letter of endorsement, they will send a recommendation for your pass to Major J. H. Carrington. He is the Provost Marshall of Richmond and the one that issues permits to leave the Confederacy to travel north."

Sarah bought the ticket to Richmond. When she reached the senators at their office near the Capitol building of the Confederacy, she explained that her mother...a French woman...was living in New York City and was in poor health. She did not hesitate to allude to the high social position of her in-laws. She stressed that her husband was even then fighting for the South. She suspected telling the senators that two of her brothers were deserters was not a good idea, especially since she wanted them to believe that her motive for going to New York was to be with her elderly mother. Thus, Sarah lied and said she had lost her only brother while he was fighting for the Confederacy. The senators asked her to wait while they conferred. When they returned, they asked Sarah where she would be staying while she awaited authorization for a ticket. Remembering the Spottswood Hotel she had passed on the way to the senators' office, Sarah gave the name. She prayed her dwindling funds would afford the accommodation.

Confederate Capitol, Richmond, Va.

While she was settling into the hotel, the senators composed a joint letter to send to Carrington stating the facts she had provided and recommending that she be permitted to continue to New York.

Not wanting to commit himself to the request in case she was a spy, Major Carrington sent the letter up the chain of command to Secretary of War, James Seddon. Seddon had turned in his resignation two weeks previous and would be leaving on February 6. Carrington figured if the woman was suspect, Seddon had less to lose than he.

Customs Building, Richmond, Va.

The next morning Sarah obeyed the order to report to Secretary of War Seddon's office in the Custom House, a handsome Italianate building on the corner of Main Street. She was frightened by the summons to appear before such an important man and was puzzled that her request had been forwarded to such a high official. Surely, she was not that important. She could not afford to appear intimidated. If they denied her request and with her remaining money only enough for the ticket to New York, what was she to do if her mother would not take her in? When she walked into Seddon's outer office, she had steeled her nerves. She had no choice, she had to convince the man to let her go to New York.

The Secretary of War, a former state representative in the U.S. congress, had far more important things on his mind than travel passes. He was in the middle of a fiasco. Jefferson Davis had established offices in Canada to encourage the Copperheads who were Union sympathizers in Indiana, Ohio, and other northern areas, to support efforts to harass northern border states and eventually break away from the Union and create a Northwestern Confederacy. Jacob Thompson, former U.S. senator and Secretary of the Interior under President Buchanan...a lawyer, statesman, and loyal Confederate... accepted the assignment to operate the offices in Toronto and Montreal. Using the astronomical sum of one million dollars, Thompson's mission was to fund and organize incursions into New England and the northern Mid-Western States from a sympathetic Canada.

The North Carolina born Jacob Thompson had an interesting history. While he was serving as a representative from Mississippi in the U.S. congress, he had the occasion to visit Peyton Jones, a wealthy Mississippi planter. Jones's daughter Catherine Anne called Kate, at fourteen years of age, was already renowned for her beauty. Thompson immediately fell for her and was determined to win her hand before he returned to Washington for fear some other man would claim her. Because of her youth, and despite the fact Kate was receptive to Jacob's proposal, Peyton Jones, declined the offer saying Kate was too young and untutored to be the wife and hostess of an important congressman. Not to be rebuffed, Thompson persisted. When he offered to marry her and delay consummation of the marriage until she was eighteen, send her to Paris to be educated, and build her a palatial home in Mississippi, Jones knew a good deal when he heard it. After a couple of years abroad, Kate returned from Europe. She and Jacob married on December 18, 1843 and moved to Washington. There she became a social sensation renowned for her polish and beauty. With the outbreak of war, they returned to their twenty-room mansion in Oxford, Mississippi. When President Jefferson Davis summoned Jacob to go to Canada, Jacob reluctantly left Kate and their son Macon behind.

For Seddon, the latest news from Montreal was a disaster putting not only Jacob Thompson, but the entire operation in peril. The raid to rob the banks in St. Albans, Vermont, did not go as planned despite seizing over two hundred thousand dollars in U.S. currency and gold. Angry villagers chased the twenty-one Confederate raiders across the Canadian border. Seven of the raiders escaped, but the remaining fourteen were apprehended by Canadian troops saving them from a lynching by the angry St. Albans citizens' posse. The fourteen men were promptly arrested and transported to Montreal for trial. In Washington, growing agitation to invade Canada to protect Union interests was growing, leaving Lincoln no choice, but to demand in no uncertain terms, return of the money and gold, immediate extradition of the culprits, and a cessation of Canadian support for Confederate incursions. If extradited for trial in the U.S., the fourteen men would be hung. With documents to prove it was an ordered military raid by a country at war with the U.S., the raiders would fall under the protection of the Webster-Ashburton Treaty.   Adjourning the trial on January 11, the judge in Montreal, James Smith, allowed a month for the prisoners to procure the necessary documents. The clock was ticking.

Seddon stood to greet Sarah as she walked into his office. Sarah sized him up. He was gaunt to the point of looking frail, with deep-set eyes that seem to pierce her.   His intent stare was unnerving as was the lack of any welcome expression on his face. Forcing herself to remain calm, Sarah ventured a smile.

"Thank you for seeing me, Mr. Secretary."

"Yes, about that. I have a request that you be permitted to pass through enemy lines to travel to New York City. With our Nation at war with our northern enemy, this is not something we take lightly. Please be seated, Mrs. Slater. I need to ask you a few questions."

Sarah sat in front of his desk. He resumed his seat behind it.

Seddon continued to study her for long minutes while Sarah forced herself not to fidget. If she was who she pretended to be, he wondered if he could use her. He needed a courier with a fresh face to carry vital documents to Canada. The most pressing matter at hand was preventing the extradition of the St. Albans raiders. He had ten days remaining to get the documents to Montreal.

The woman in front of him was no more than twenty-two years of age, and not only lovely, but coolly self-possessed. With a crown of thick curly black hair, blue eyes, perfect features, and a voluptuous figure she was a woman to turn heads. Beautiful young women had proven to be ideal couriers as they were given far more leniency from suspicious inspection than any man. Noting that her mother was French, Seddon decided to test her.

Although he knew some French, he was far from fluent, but it was enough for him to challenge her claims of a French mother. Switching from English to French to flummox her if she were lying, he noted that she never flinched but calmly responded in perfect and fluent French. Seddon picked up the letter from the senators and pretended to study it. Sarah sat quietly and waited for what felt like an eternity.

"Mrs. Slater, I have a proposition for you. If you are willing, you will be provided for handsomely...two hundred dollars in gold to cover your expenses and payment for your services. With agents to conduct you by carriage and see to your lodging, your expenses will be modest leaving only the expense of railway tickets." He noted the sudden flare of interest in her eyes before she looked down. Oh, yes, he thought, the money interests her. With Confederate currency increasingly worthless, two hundred in gold would be a fortune to Mrs. Slater. "I need a woman with your attributes to serve as a courier to our office in Canada. You will be well paid for each of the trips that you make to Canada. If for some reason you should be apprehended, you can always claim French citizenship and appeal to French diplomatic services for help. There is no reason to anticipate that you will be stopped; however, it is always useful to have a convincing fallback."

Sarah met his eyes but did not respond.

"Mrs. Slater, as the wife of a Confederate soldier, the sister of a man that gave his life to our cause, can I trust you? Or do your sympathies lie with the North where you were born?"

For Sarah, it was the now or never moment. She did not give a damn for either side of this stupid war. If Seddon was willing to pay her that kind of money to run some errands that appeared to present little or no personal risk, why shouldn't she do it? She was all but broke, and the money was more than appealing. Thinking about the best response, she sat with her hands in her lap and her head bowed. Sarah smiled as she lifted her head, her eyes glistening with the unshed tears she had always been able to summon at will and met his steady regard.

"Secretary Seddon, I am honored that you would consider me a worthy person to help our noble cause. Although the North is where I was born, except for my mother, my family is in the South and my husband is risking his life for the Confederacy. If by doing this for you, I can help him and the South in some small way…no matter how indirectly, I will do so."

Seddon silently applauded the performance. He had his courier. "Thank you, Mrs. Slater. I will tell you what you need to know, if you will give me some more of your time. Then you can be on your way north. You may visit your mother briefly during your time in New York, but you may not linger."

"I understand."

Sarah sat quietly as he fleshed out the Canadian enterprise and the procedures that were in place for a courier. When he had finished, he pulled open the bottom left drawer on his desk and extracted a leather pouch containing the promised gold. He stood and handed a sealed packet and the pouch to his new courier. She reached for it, a satisfied smile on her face. For a moment he wondered if he would ever see her again…or if his gold, the packet, and along with them, Mrs. Slater would vanish. As insurance, he reminded her that she would be paid in gold for each trip she took to Toronto. Hopefully, that would be inducement enough to guarantee her delivery of the letter and her return.

Unbeknownst to her, the wily Seddon was not putting all his eggs in her basket. For Mrs. Slater this was a test run to see if she would be a reliable courier. Seddon also sent Reverend Stephen Cameron, a reliable courier, with a duplicate set of the documents carried by Sarah. It was Cameron that would testify at the extradition hearing in Montreal leaving Mrs. Slater anonymous.

Sarah took the gold and immediately went shopping. She had no intention of anyone seeing her face on the journey and thus be able to identify her afterwards. She bought a well-cut black silk dress with black velvet bands, a black hat with a heavy veil, and black gloves. The dress showed her curves to advantage, she noted with pleasure, while the hat and veil made it impossible to see her face and hair with any real discernment of features. On January 31, 1865…a cold, dismal Tuesday remembered afterward as the day the U.S. House of Representatives passed the bill freeing all slaves, Sarah left Richmond with a male escort. He did not give his name and she did not give hers.

At the Richmond depot, the escort bought two tickets on the recently reopened Richmond, Fredericksburg, and Potomac Railroad. Using the well-organized route for Confederate couriers, mail, and agents, they arrived at Milford Station, in Virginia. From there they traveled by carriage to Bowling Green and on to Port Royal. In Port Royal they boarded the Rappahannock River ferry that would carry them to the Confederate signal corps camp near the mouth of Mattox Creek. The camp was in Westmoreland County on the Virginia side of the river.

Here the routes for the Confederate blockader runners diverged. One choice was a ferry across the river to the Maryland side, landing at Swan Point in Charles County. Other landing sites were in the Chaptico area and in St. Mary's County. Beginning in Leonardtown, a stage line ran through Chaptico, Charlotte Hall, Bryantown, T. B., Surrattsville, and from there to Washington. Confederate loyalists would pick up some couriers in Chaptico and carry them north. Along the route, there were safe houses where they could be fed, sheltered, and escorted onward.

The other option, reserved mostly for mail, branched off from Port Royal and ran to the small signal corps camp near Mathias Point close to the mouth of Machodoc Creek in King George County. From there they were taken by boat to various points in the Pope's Creek and Port Tobacco areas of Maryland. They then traveled from Port Tobacco to Washington by way of Bumpy Oak, T. B., and Surrattsville.

The Maryland portion of the route was operated by a group of Seccessionist Maryland physicians, earning it the moniker "the doctor's line." Despite repeated Federalist attempts to shut down the line of transportation through Maryland, it continued to operate with little hinderance as the Yankee troops in the sparsely populated area made only half-hearted and sporadic attempts to quash their activities.

When they reached the Mattox Creek camp on February 1, the escort handed Sarah off to Augustus Howell. Called Gus, the twenty-seven-year old Howell, had been arrested several times but remained an expert guide. Following his last arrest, he had been required to take the oath of allegiance to the United States to gain parole. A staunch supporter of the Confederacy, Howell had no hesitation about taking the oath, nor any compunction about immediately resuming his activities.

Gus Howell was instantly attracted to the beautiful woman

that he would take to New York. Despite repeated attempts at flirtation, the aloof Sarah refused to tell him more than her name, 'Mrs. Slater.' When pressed for answers, she responded in broken English with a pronounced French accent. Frequently she replied in French with a shrug of her shoulders as though she could not understand him. That did nothing to lessen his admiration for the exotic widow, although it added considerably to his frustration that he could make no headway with her during the days they were together.

In New York, she insisted that he leave her in front of the European Hotel where Howell would spend one or two days before going south to Washington.

Refusing, to accept defeat, Howell tried one last time. "Mrs. Slater, please permit me to escort you to dinner. The food in the hotel is quite good."

"No, thank you." Sarah used the heavy accent and broken English to add, "My mother I go to see."

Gus watched the woman hail a hansom cab. He could not hear the address she gave. There was a momentary glimpse of a shapely ankle when she climbed in the cab. Oh, well, he decided, if she continued as a courier, they would cross paths again and perhaps the next time his pursuit of her would prove more fortuitous.

Sarah had mixed feelings about seeing her mother but felt obligated to make a brief visit. She had not seen her since they left Hartford that early morning over four years past. Much had happened to her since then and to her brothers. She had no idea if Antoinette knew of Frederick's death or if she had heard from Eugene and Robert since they deserted from the camp outside Kinston.

Sarah alit from the cab and looked around her. Looking down at the slip of paper she held, she checked to make sure that she had the correct address. She did not expect to find her mother living in an affluent neighborhood, but Becton Street...on the lower side of Manhattan, in the middle of squalid tenements, and near the wharves...was a shock to her sensibilities.

"Are you sure this is the right address, ma'am?" the Cabbie asked.

"I think so." She was terrified he would leave before she was certain her mother lived here. "Would you wait for me, please? I won't be long, then I need to find a hotel for the night."

"It will cost you. I can't afford to sit here for nothing."

"I understand."

"Don't be long, ma'am. This ain't the best place to hang out."

"No, no. I promise...just a few minutes."

Sarah walked up the steps of the tenement and entered the foyer. On the right, wooden stairs ascended to the gloom of upper floors. Her mother's apartment was on the third floor. Sarah wondered if she still lived there. Sarah climbed the dusty steps, pausing before knocking briskly on the flaking door of her mother's apartment. When there was no answer, she rapped again. A minute or so later, she could hear movement within. Another minute passed. The door opened a crack and a querulous voice demanded, "Who's there?"

"Maman, it's me, Nettie."

Recognizing Sarah's voice, Antoinette swung the door open. Sarah found herself staring at Antoinette. Her mother had aged from the youthful beauty of her portrait into an old and slovenly woman. Sarah wanted to embrace her mother, to feel some love and welcome from her, but Antoinette held herself rigid with her arms crossed in front.

Hating the awkwardness of the moment, Sarah asked, "May I come in?"

Antoinette stepped back as Sarah entered, studying the elegantly dressed woman that stood before her. "Take off that veil so I can see your face."

Sarah lifted the veil over her hat. "Is that better?"

"My goodness, Nettie, you have grown into a beautiful woman. You look a lot like I did at your age. It looks like you are doing right well for yourself, too." Taking note of Sarah's attire, she inquired, "For whom are you wearing mourning?"

Sarah was not about to explain the necessity of the widow's weeds, saying instead, "Did you hear that Frederick died of measles almost two years ago now?"

"Lord, my baby boy. So many of my children have died." Her face was etched with grief. Antoinette had always shown far more partiality and affection to her sons than to Sarah.

"Tell me...Eugene, Robert are they well?"

"To tell the truth, Maman, I don't know."

Antoinette cried, "What do you mean?"

"Eugene got into some trouble and he and Robert took off for parts unknown. I hoped you would have heard from them."

Her mother shook her head, "No, nothing from either one of them. Last I heard from any of you was when Robert wrote to say all my boys were in the Confederate army."

After a moment, Antoinette demanded, "Well, what about your father?"

"I have not heard from him since I left Goldsboro in July of 1863."

"I see." Antoinette glanced at Sarah's finger. "I don't see any wedding band, so I guess you are still unwed."

Sarah merely smiled without bothering to correct her. "I have to leave now. I'm sorry I can't stay any longer."

Antoinette shrugged as if it made no difference. Sarah assumed it probably didn't. As she turned to leave, she looked around the dingy apartment and was glad her work for Seddon gave her an option besides moving in with her mother.

Sarah turned around to face her mother and asked, "How do you support yourself? I think it can't be easy."

"Easy? When has my life ever been easy? Certainly, not since I left Martinique... As for supporting myself, I sew lace and do fine finish work for a local clothing factory. They let me work from home. I prefer it this way compared to working alongside that slatternly bunch of Irish women at the factory. The pay isn't much. I suppose a good look at this place will tell you that. I also give French lessons from time to time. I haven't taught piano since moving to New York."

"Have you considered returning to Middletown? Father has a lot of relatives there. Surely one of them would take you in."

"That bridge is burned."

For an instant, Sarah wanted to suggest her mother reunite with her husband but didn't. If Joseph were her husband instead of her father, Sarah wouldn't go back to him either.

Feeling sorry for her mother, she fished twenty dollars in gold from her reticule and pressed it into Antoinette's hand. "I will try to send you more from time to time."

"I would appreciate it. My life here is not an easy one."

BLOCKADE RUNNING
Chapter 8

Sarah reached Montreal in the small hours of the morning on February 15, 1865. By the time she checked into the St. Lawrence Hall Hotel and registered as Mrs. N. Slater of New York, it was three in the morning. She was beyond tired but made it a point to awaken at six in order to dress and turn the documents she carried over to Jacob Thompson first thing. Thompson had made the St. Lawrence his residence and office headquarters for the Canada Cabinet of the Confederacy. He kept a suite of rooms for the use of his staff and visiting couriers in this, the most luxurious hotel in Montreal. Sarah was unaware that Reverend Stephen Cameron had arrived on February 14 with a duplicate set of the very records she carried. Thompson received Sarah's packet when she arrived in the hotel dining room and was directed to his table where he was enjoying a hearty breakfast.

He was impressed by the petite woman whose quick wit and charm were valuable assets in her line of work. "Did you encounter any difficulties in your journey here, Mrs. Slater?"

"Thank you for asking. Other than the discomfort of travel, I was fine."

He took the package she handed across the table and opened it. After riffling through the papers, he commented, "Mr. Seddon enclosed a note in the packet saying that this is your first trip for the Confederacy. As he may have mentioned, we were in serious need of a new face to run this route. He mentions that your unexpected fluency in French is fortuitous for both of us as it provides a ready rationale for your trips to Montreal. I am going to provide you with an address here so you can claim residency should you be challenged during your travels for us."

St. Lawrence Hall, Montreal, Canada

Handing her the menu, he told her to order. While Sarah arranged her breakfast, Thompson studied the attractive woman across the table. When he returned to his food, she took time to do some perusing of her own. His strong features made him a compelling man, but his commanding presence even more so. This was a man accustomed to getting his way.

After some pondering on whether to give the next mission to Cameron or Mrs. Slater, he decided to use Cameron in Montreal, and have Sarah carry to Richmond an urgent missive to Secretary of State, Judah Benjamin. The St. Albans raid and the aftermath of the raiders' capture had created a political nightmare for him with the Canadian government. Thompson had reason to fear they would charge him with violating Canada's neutrality. He needed someone to relieve him before he could be arrested.

His decision made: he would instruct Cameron to turn over to the Montreal court the documents Seddon had provided him to carry stating that the raiders were acting under military orders. Thus, Cameron would be the one to testify before Judge Smith. The documents and Cameron's testimony would prove decisive, leaving Smith no choice but to refuse extradition of the St. Albans raiders under the terms of the Webster-Ashburton Treaty. With the documents from Richmond proving their claim, the judge freed the defendants and turned over the money stolen during the raid to Thompson as the authorized agent of the Confederate government.

With Thompson stressing the urgency of the dispatches he was giving her to carry, Sarah would have little opportunity to explore Montreal as she had to leave the following morning. She had only the remainder of that day to enjoy lingering on the streets of Montreal. French speaking citizens milled around her on the street making her feel at home in the city. Unable to resist a particularly appealing shop with a tempting display of women's apparel, Sarah pushed open the door and entered. A bell over the door announced her presence bringing the shop owner bustling through a curtain in the rear to greet her. Soon Sarah was drooling over the latest of fashions. In a spirit of profligacy, she tried on a green silk dress with a low décolleté. Admiring herself in the mirror, she could not resist what it did for her figure. She could never have afforded, nor dared to wear such an elegant dress in the war-torn South where women were wearing their patched and faded pre-war dresses with defiant pride.

She decided to wear her new dress to supper in the hotel dining room rather than her widow's weeds. When she walked in, every man in the room turned to stare at the beautiful young woman. Holding her head as proudly as any queen, Sarah walked to Thompson's table. He and the other men with him immediately arose. Momentarily non-plussed by her uninvited presence, Thompson ordered a chair for Mrs. Slater, then introduced her to Clement Clay. Clay, the former senator from Alabama, was serving as the Commissioner of the North. He then introduced James Holcombe, a University of Virginia Law Professor, Brigadier General Edwin Lee the ranking Confederate military officer in Canada, and Captain Thomas Hines who appeared to be around Sarah's age.

She would learn later that Hines, despite his youth, was an ardent but overly enthusiastic and optimistic spy for the Confederacy. His zeal led him to be too trusting, thus thwarting many of his endeavors when they were exposed by Union spies in his midst. With Sarah at the table, the men dropped their previous discussion and set about charming her. They succeeded so well that Sarah was hoping to be assigned to return to Montreal on another mission. Despite the flattering attention, she made it a point to respond to none of the flirtatious remarks Hines aimed her way. The other men were married and careful to keep their attention to a polite social level despite their open admiration. At the conclusion of the meal, Thompson discretely reminded Sarah that she had an early morning train to catch. He slipped her the train ticket and the packet she was to deliver to Judah Benjamin, Secretary of State, as she stood to leave the table.

Watching her leave, Thompson remarked, "Seddon certainly picked a beauty for our new courier."

Captain Hines added, "I wouldn't mind Seddon sending her on another mission to Canada. I'd like to get to know that lady better."

Holcombe chuckled before quipping, "Let's hope you will be on another mission of your own that is more successful than the last one we sent you on...when and if she returns."

Thompson interjected, "As for our lovely new courier, she strikes me as a cool one despite the undeniably provocative attire. I gather she has a husband fighting in our army, so you might chase after someone a little less married and a little bit warmer to your attentions."

Hines blushed as the others laughed. The other men had all watched in amusement as she adroitly handled the blatantly smitten Captain in his every attempt to gain her interest.

Sarah left at dawn the following day retracing her route by rail back to New York where Thompson had arranged for her to meet John Surratt, a native of Washington and an ardent supporter of the Confederacy. Surratt was assigned to escort her from New York to Washington.

Prior to Sarah's arrival in New York, Surratt had visited in the upscale home of the Edwin Booths in Greenwich Village where Edwin's brother, J. Wilkes Booth, was visiting. Aside from his political interests, John Wilkes Booth was one of the most prominent actors of his day, celebrated for his ability on the stage, but also for his Byronic looks making him the heartthrob of many women, both northern and southern. With a lusty appreciation of the opposite sex, J. Wilkes enjoyed a varied love life. He came from a family of actors as his brother Edwin and their father were the most celebrated Shakespearean performers of their day. The Maryland-born J. Wilkes and Johnny Surrat were well-known to one another and actively involved in clandestine activities on behalf of the Confederacy.

When the two men met, Surratt told Booth that he was charged with escorting a new female courier from New York to Washington where another escort would meet her and take her by buggy to the crossing point on the Potomac River. Surratt needed a horse and buggy for the trip from Washington to the Potomac crossing. With a residence in the National Hotel in Washington, Booth kept both horse and buggy at the nearby Howard's Livery Stable. He agreed to loan them to the female courier and her escort with the understanding that another man would go with them by horse and return the buggy to Howard's Livery.

Surratt met Sarah in front of a hotel on Broadway. Sarah was cold, tired, and hungry and Surratt was late from his meeting with Booth. After acknowledging a pre-arranged signal, Sarah introduced herself to Surratt who was instantly smitten by her looks. On the way to the railway station, she felt his eyes constantly on her. When she caught him ogling her bosom, he wasted no time looking away and making some inane comment. Sarah was not impressed. The man was slim, with non-descript brown hair that appeared to be thinning, a scraggly beard on a weak chin, and pale eyes. There was nothing about him that inspired a similar infatuation in Sarah. To avoid conversation, she pretended to sleep for much of the rail trip from New York to Washington.

Undaunted by her silence, John talked about his family endlessly despite nothing more than an occasional murmur from Sarah. She could tell by his comments that he was fond of his sister Anna who helped his mother run the boarding house. He told Sarah that both women were devout Catholics. His mother owned both the townhouse where they were now living and a tavern in Surrattsville. When his father, the local postmaster died…leaving them in debt due to his gambling, his mother rented the tavern and moved to the townhouse where she rented rooms to make ends meet. John Surratt took over his father's postmaster duties giving John the perfect excuse for his travels in the sparsely populated area of lower Maryland used by Confederate couriers. Hoping to impress her, he could not help boasting about several of his exploits. Sarah suspected his role was heavily embellished with exaggerations.

Annoyed at having been kept waiting for him in New York, Sarah ignored him and avoided speaking to Surratt unless necessary. Due to a deficit of sleep while in Montreal, she soon drifted off despite the discomfort of the train. Surratt studied her sleeping form for a time before he too slept. On arrival in Washington, John collected Booth's horse and buggy and went back for Sarah who was waiting at the station. It was almost dusk on February 22 when they reached the boarding house at 541 H Street NW, Washington, owned by John's mother, Mary Surratt. There, Gus Howell was waiting to escort Sarah to Richmond.

When they pulled up to the boarding house, Howell immediately came out of the Surratt home and exchanged places with John Surratt. Sarah could tell John was reluctant to turn over his place in the buggy to the better-looking Augustus Howell. It mattered nothing to her. Her insipid husband, after a domineering and self-centered father, had done nothing to encourage any real appreciation for the male sex. Somewhere along her path since leaving Hartford, and with Robert her childhood confidant gone, Sarah had determined to rely on nothing but herself. For a moment, she was saddened that she no longer appreciated male attention other than as flattery to her vanity. She was not one of those women that enjoyed the company of women either. Sarah suspected she was becoming a loner. In her role as courier, perhaps that was better.

They left Washington in the Booth buggy with George Atzerodt, a boarder at Mary Surrat's home, riding alongside on horseback. After Howell and Sarah crossed the Potomac to Port Royal, Atzerodt would return to Washington with the buggy and horses. When they arrived on the outskirts of Port Tobacco they were joined by James Fowle, son of an Episcopal Clergyman. It was Fowle's job to meet Gus Howell, Atzerodt and Sarah and lead them to a local safe house to spend the night.

Port Tobacco lies around an old canal close to the point where Tobacco Creek enters the broad estuary of the Potomac River. Founded in 1634, it was a proud old town, that was once the second largest port in Maryland. In recent years, the creek had begun to silt up reducing the size of the ships that could use its harbor. Nearby creeks and inlets created the perfect haven for clandestine crossings. Many families in the area had large plantations worked by slaves and were sympathetic to the Southern cause.

It was late when Fowle led Sarah, Howell, and Atzerodt to their destination, a large two-story brick Georgian plantation home surrounded by 600 acres of land that sat on a hill just outside of town. Rose Hill was home to the elderly Sarah Semmes Floyd and her thirty-nine-year old daughter, Olivia, a lame, hunch-backed spinster. Olivia wore the black of mourning for her younger brother, Robert, who had died two years previously while fighting for the Confederacy under General Jeb Stuart. His death had only increased Olivia's passion for the Southern cause. The Yankees, suspecting she was involved in clandestine activities for the Confederates, had yet to catch the shrewd woman despite numerous attempts.

Following a tip that something was going on, a Yankee search party had invaded her home several weeks before. She outwitted them by hiding documents from Canada that she had just received in the hollow tops of huge brass fireirons in her dining room fireplace. With a roaring blaze in the fireplace, the Yankees ignored the hot andirons as they searched the house. Indeed, the officer that queried her as his soldiers ransacked the house, sat on a hassock by the fire with his feet resting on one of those very andirons. The next morning, with the two pistols she always carried concealed in the pockets of her dress and the message hidden in the curls of her hair, Olivia rode her horse to the Confederate signal station at Pope's Creek, where it was then delivered to Richmond. Those were the very documents that alerted Seddon to the situation in Montreal following the St.

Albans raid. And it was the reason that Sarah now found herself at Olivia's home.

Rose Hill, Port Tobacco, Maryland

Informed in advance by Fowle to expect company, Olivia met them on the dark porch of the mansion with a warning hiss to be quiet. Olivia Floyd, aware she was being closely watched, was wary of anything that might signal the Yankee patrol of what was afoot that night. The feisty spinster had been lucky so far. But who knew what small slip would cause her luck to run out?

Fowle gave Olivia the password and introduced her to the two people with him, before fading into the night-darkened forest behind the woman's house. Inviting Sarah and the men inside, Olivia led them down a dark foyer to a stairway. Their only light was the shielded candle she carried. They followed silently, being careful not to trip, as they ascended to the second floor. There she led them to a doorway, unlocked the door, and again they climbed. She handed them each a candle that she lit from the one she carried. She directed Sarah to a room on the right side of the attic and Howell and Atzerodt to a chamber on the opposite side.

Olivia, her voice raspy and high-pitched, told them she would have food and water brought up by a servant. She warned them that if the Yankees were to raid, they were to take their candle and hide in the large chests they would find in each room being careful to extinguish their candles once they were hidden under the blankets they would find there. When they finished eating, they were instructed to put their dishes in the chests where one of her servants would collect them when they left. They were to leave nothing in the room during the night to indicate their presence in the event of a raid. She told them to stash their bags in the chests once they had whatever they might need for the night to prevent inadvertently leaving something out that would give them away should the Yankees come.

Olivia Floyd followed Sarah into the room she was assigned for the night to thank her for her help in getting messages back and forth to Canada. She lit a candle for Sarah on the one small table and taking the candle she had given Sarah, stuck it in a sconce on the wall. Next, the diminutive woman pointed out the chest and the narrow bed where Sarah would sleep. The remainder of the room was a hodge-podge of years of cobweb festooned cast-offs, trunks, and old toys. One heavily draped window concealed any light from the outside. For the casual observer, it looked like nothing more than an abandoned room for servants.

"I am sorry I cannot offer you more pleasant accommodation, but the danger of being caught helping Southern blockade runners is great. They have been harassing me for a couple of years now, but that hasn't stopped me any in trying to help the South when I can."

"This is fine. I'm so tired it will make no difference what the room is like."

"As a security measure should the patrol come, the door at the bottom of the stairs will be locked once you have your suppers. Be careful with that candle. If you start a fire, we could not get you out in time."

"Yes, of course." Sarah did not like the idea of being locked in with Gus Howell just across the stair landing, but what could she do?

Olivia told her goodnight and left. Sarah could hear her say something to someone at the foot of the stairs. Soon steps announced someone coming her way. The smell of food anticipated the arrival of servants with trays bearing a covered dish, a goblet of wine, and a pitcher of water all covered by a towel. One of the women knocked on Howell's door. The other knocked on Sarah's, silently placed the tray on the small table, and left.

Wasting not a moment, Sarah removed her hat and veil and fell on the food. She was so ravenous she picked up the piece of ham and gnawed on it, ignoring the fork and knife that lay beside the plate. Its salty pungency was delicious. Next, she peeled the top off a warm sweet potato using the unpeeled end to stuff it into her mouth. She was glad there was no one to observe her lack of manners. Lastly, with biscuits a rarity due to the dearth of flour, there was a slab of the ubiquitous cornbread. Such homely fare had never tasted so good. Thirstily she drank the wine and then poured a goblet of water and drank that, too. Sarah could only grin at the contrast when she recalled the elegant meal she had enjoyed in the hotel in Montreal and the dashing silk dress she had worn. Finished with the food, she removed her black widow's garb, underskirts, and corset. It was a relief to be free of the constricting corset that forced her to sit rigidly erect and take only shallow breaths. Wearing her chemise, Sarah poured another glass of water into the goblet, and then using the towel from the tray, dipped it into the cold water to sponge off as best she could. Sarah was shivering long before she finished her ablutions. She thought with longing of sitting in a hot bath as she had done in Montreal. There her room had been furnished with the luxury of a private bath and hotel supplied bath salts. This drab attic room offered no such comforts.

She put the tray and dishes into one end of the chest and her carefully folded clothes in the other. Then she added her valise. With that done, she looked around the room to assure that none of her belongings were left out should she be forced to hide. Folding back the blankets, she sat on the edge of the narrow cot for only a moment before wrapping up. Despite the chimneys that ran up one wall providing some radiant heat from the bricks, the room was icy cold. It was a long time before she could warm up enough to fall into a restless sleep.

That night she dreamed she was dancing in an elegant ballroom in her green silk gown while her brothers Eugene and Robert stood on the sidelines in immaculate evening attire waiting for the dance to end. Diamonds sparkled at her ears as she tossed her head in flirtation, teasing the man that held her. She could not see his face as they swirled to the music, but she could sense that he was handsome. When the dance ended, she tried to thank him for the dance, but he had faded into a mist. A little sad that she had to leave the dancer behind, Sarah joined her brother and the three of them walked through the ballroom door onto a pier. There a steamship awaited to bear them off into the dark night. In her dream she found herself struggling to remember where the ship was taking them. It was their new home, but she could not say where it was…only that it was French.

DIRE PROSPECTS
Chapter 9

During the night, thick fingers of fog wrapped themselves around the trees, thickets, and waterways of Port Tobacco. On the hill, the brick mansion sat above it all like an island in a sea of gray. Pulling the heavy cloth from the window, Sarah peered out into the early morning gloom. She wondered if they would be forced to stay until the fog cleared. She was standing at the window when a knock sounded on her door. Letting the curtain fall, she called out, "Yes?"

"I gots you breakfus iffn you up."

"Yes, please. Come in."

Sarah smiled at the woman who delivered her tray. She recognized her from the evening before. The elderly servant stood back once she had set the tray on the table and told Sarah, "Miss Olivia say be ready to go soon."

"Yes, thank you. I'll do that."

After the woman left, Sarah tasted the coffee made from Okra seeds and sweetened with honey. It was a far cry from what people were drinking in the North, especially in Montreal. Breakfast was cold cornbread and buttermilk. It was not something she liked, but not knowing how long it would be before the next opportunity to eat, she forced it down. She finished the ersatz coffee and hastened to retrieve her clothing from the chest and prepare for another day on the road. She had just donned the hat and veil when Gus Howell knocked on her door.

"Mr. Atzerodt is getting the horse hitched up. I expect we better get going before the fog lifts. I want to be away from here before folks start stirring. This area is always crawling with Yankees, and they are suspicious of Miss Olivia. Until we can find a better safe house, this is the best we can do, but I sure don't like it none."

"Just a moment, Mr. Howell. I'm almost ready." Sarah dropped the pretense of speaking with him in broken French. He had been with her in Judah Benjamin's office when she had spoken fluent English. Although he now realized she could understand every word he was saying, she hoped her continued use of his last name would imply no interest in greater familiarity.

Sarah hurriedly stuffed the last of her things in her valise. The documents were securely lodged under her corset; her hat and veil were in place. At the last moment, she decided to use the chamber pot again before leaving. It was embarrassing to have to stop a male escort on route in order to hike into the woods when her bladder became uncomfortable. At least if she peed now, it would be awhile before she needed to stop again. Hopefully, Howell did not have his ear pressed to her door to hear her relieve herself.

Brushing her skirt into place, Sarah turned to survey the room to be sure she had everything. Satisfied, she joined Howell on the landing. The door at the bottom of the stairs framed the figure of Olivia Floyd who was waving impatiently.

"Hurry. The other gentleman has your horse and buggy waiting out back. If y'all get going now while the fog is thick, you should be well away before it clears."

Both Sarah and Howell thanked the woman as they scurried

out the door. From the interior of the house, Sarah heard a tremulous voice demanding, "Olivia, who in the world is out there this time of the morning? I swaney the goings on around here. You mark my words, Olivia..."

The spinster interrupted the coming tirade, "It's no one mother. I was just talking to the servants. If you are ready for breakfast, I will have it brought in."

The door closed behind them, preventing Sarah or Gus Howell from hearing any more. They walked to the back of the house where Atzerodt was already astride his horse and holding the reins of the one hitched to the buggy. Howell helped Sarah into the buggy before walking to the other side and clambering in. Taking up the reins from Atzerodt, he snapped them smartly against the horse's back. The fog had wet the leaves around the house muffling the sound of the horses' hooves and the buggy's wheels as they left Rose Hill. All three were content to immerse themselves in their own thoughts as they drove into the gloom of the day. By mid-morning, the fog had been replaced by a damp drizzle that seemed to soak into every pore and crevasse.

Several miles from town the sound of numerous horses and jangling harnesses alerted them to a Yankee patrol. Leaving the road hurriedly, they sat under trees surrounded by dense undergrowth that hid them from view. Sarah was miserable, the weather making the trip feel interminable. Judging by the grim set of his mouth, Howell was no happier about the delay than they were. At least, for the moment he was too intent on avoiding Yankees to try flirting with her. Atzerodt didn't look any more thrilled they were. After thirty dreary minutes, Howell told Atzerodt that it seemed safe to continue.

When they finally reached the waiting boat near Great Goose

Creek, the sun began to burn off the fog, making the day less oppressive. Atzerodt tied the horses to a tree branch and pulled the boat out of the weeds on the edge of the shore. After rowing them across to Mathias Point, he waved Sarah and Howell off as he turned the boat around for the return trip. Howell procured another horse and buggy from the livery stable at Mathias Point.

Livery stable

When they reached, Milford Station, they left the horse and buggy at the nearby livery and purchased tickets to Richmond. Settling into their seats on the train, they both breathed a sigh of relief that they had not been stopped by the Yankees while traversing Maryland. If caught, Howell risked hanging as a spy and Sarah would be faced with imprisonment if she were stripped and the documents found. She took comfort in the fact that thus far no women had been hung in the United States. Even the celebrated Confederate spy, Belle Boyd had been released during a prisoner exchange. The same leniency was not shown to male spies.

It was late when they arrived in Richmond. Sarah checked

into the Spottswood Hotel she had used previously. There she had letters waiting. When she had stayed in the hotel prior to going to Canada, she had written to her in-laws letting them know she was in Richmond and hoping to be allowed to go to her mother in New York. In the meantime, she asked them to forward any mail that arrived for her to her hotel. She had three letters: one was from her father, one from her husband, and one from her in-laws. After a quick meal of cold leftovers in the hotel dining room, Sarah gathered her letters from the table and climbed the stairs to the second floor.

Sarah, photo courtesy of Jane Clancy

When she reached her room, she opened the letter from Rowan first. He told her that he was with Lee, and things were looking grim for the South. He described how he and his fellow soldiers marched onward to inevitable defeat accompanied by nothing but lost hope, hunger, and the scourge of lice. He had given up hope as had so many and was praying daily for it all to be behind him. Like most of his other letters, this one dwelt on the end of the war and picking up their lives in his hometown. Sarah knew that no matter what he said or promised she would never return to Salisbury. Pushing his letter to one side, she picked up the one from her mother-in-law. The letter was as sour as the woman in person, berating Sarah for her ingratitude and for leaving without a word. Without bothering to finish the diatribe, Sarah ripped the letter in half and threw it in the waste basket by the door.

Lastly, she picked up the letter from her father. It was brief. It was the enclosure that held her interest and made her heart beat faster. Carefully, Sarah refolded it into a tiny sliver and hid it under the hatband of her black widow's hat. Sarah sat at the small desk beside the window and wrote a short note. In the morning, she would get an envelope, address it, and ask the hotel to post it for her.

The next morning, March 3, Sarah and Howell had breakfast at her hotel before walking to the Capitol. They were immediately shown into the Secretary of State's office. Benjamin motioned to them to be seated while he read the documents she had delivered. She watched the heavy-set man's brows draw together in concentration as he read.

When Benjamin had finished, he folded the papers and laid them on his desk. He tapped them with his right forefinger as he sat lost in thought. Looking up, Benjamin studied Sarah's face for a moment. She shifted in her seat. She had no way of knowing if that intent look was because she had done something wrong on her trip to Canada for Seddon, or what it was that had him looking so somber. Sarah could think of nothing she had done, so surely it was something else. She shifted nervously in her chair as she waited for him to say something. Beside her, Howell merely looked bored and eager to leave.

His head snapped up and he barked, "Mr. Howell, I will contact you shortly. Get some rest and I'll see you then."

When Gus stood up to leave, Sarah also began to rise, "No, Mrs. Slater. I need to talk to you for a moment more."

Sarah sank back into her seat, her pulse racing. She sat in suspense until Howell had left the office and he spoke again, "Mrs. Slater, I appreciate the trouble you went to getting our message to Mr. Thompson in Montreal. The message you returned with from him, leads me to believe that it's crucial that we send a reply immediately. It is in your best interest to know nothing more than that should you be apprehended by Union troops. I realize the risk I put you in, but the situation is dire. Keeping that in mind, I am going to ask if you are willing to return to Montreal? You will be paid 200 in gold just as you were when you went for Secretary Seddon."

Sarah would have liked more than a few days to rest, but the thought of adding more gold to what she had already earned was too appealing to turn down. "Yes, of course. If you need me to go, I will."

"Good. Leave the name of your hotel with my clerk. I'll get in touch with you as soon as I can make the necessary arrangements. I should have it sorted out in a day or two at the latest."

"Yes, sir. Thank you, sir." Sarah left his office. On reaching the street, she took a big gulp of air and then grinned. She must have done well if they were hiring her for another trip so quickly after the first. She did some mental calculations. She had over

$350 in gold from the first trip after giving her mother $20 of the $400 and spending less than $30. If she could make this next trip and spend only $50, then she would have at least $700 in gold when added to what she already had, since she was paid both $200 in Richmond and another $200 in Canada...not counting the money left of what Lottie had given her. With Confederate money worthless, that amount in gold felt like a fortune.

Judah P. Benjamin was only moments behind Sarah as he hurried from his office to that of Jefferson Davis. The Confederate President was standing at the window looking out at Richmond. Without turning, he said, "I wonder what this city will look like a couple of months from now."

Not bother to respond to the comment, Judah Benjamin immediately got down to business. "Mr. President, I need to discuss the situation in Montreal if you have a moment?"

Davis felt no such urgency to deal with Montreal when so many other issues seemed more critical. "Have a seat, Mr. Benjamin. I suspect it is no better news than all the rest. It seems that I keep facing one disaster after another. As you are aware, General Sherman's troops pretty much burned South Carolina's capital to the ground February 17, after laying waste to everything in a sixty-mile wide swath from Atlanta northward. Now Charleston and Wilmington have fallen which means we cannot import much of what we need to continue waging war. That tells me General Sherman will likely go for our arsenal in Fayetteville, N.C. next. I swear that man's like a Satan from hell as he destroys the very heart and soul of our southern states. You may not have heard, but I was just notified that General George Custer defeated our troops in Waynesville. With General Sheridan's defeat of our forces in the Shenandoah, our men have burned the bridges to slow General Sherman down if he heads that way to join up with Sheridan after he finishes his destruction of the Carolinas. For all intents and purposes, we are finished in the west.

"With these latest losses, our armies are being depleted. Not only are you an advocate for allowing our Negroes to fight, but now our Generals are urging to allow them to fight in order to replace the many men that have been wounded or died. The Senate is still debating that. Despite some of you in favor of it, I've never thought much of the idea."

Refusing to be drawn into an argument, Benjamin remained silent. The freeing and empowering of the Negro was one of several points of contention between the two. It was frustrating for him that Davis had ignored so many of his recommendations which might have made a difference to the survival of the Confederate nation.

Davis continued, "As if all that were not enough, Lincoln is going to be inaugurated for another term tomorrow, and I hear he is already planning what to do when we are beaten. Not 'if,' they say...but 'when.' And yet, here we are meeting at the same time to discuss and approve a new design for our Confederate flag. I can only pray we have reason for a new flag, and General Lee can turn things around for us."

"When Lincoln flat out rejected our terms for peace last month, he must have had reason to think The Union would prevail. However, so far, despite the overwhelming strength of the North, our men have defied all odds. We must keep faith that they will find the will and means to persevere. If anyone can lead them to victory, it's Robert E. Lee." Benjamin paused, impatient to get to the matter at hand, "On the matter I need to discuss,

Jacob Thompson needs to be replaced to avoid arrest. The St. Albans fiasco has created a fine mess in Montreal. There is rumor Thompson will be indicted for violating Canadian neutrality. The political situation there is unstable as some Canadians are considering breaking away and forming an allied Confederate State in the north as a result of some of our activities there. Needless to say, we do not want to give Canada any further reason for shutting down our Canadian offices. A presence there is vital for maintaining communications with England and Europe. Therefore, I am requesting Brigadier General Edwin Lee take over for Mr. Thompson. I am hoping he can calm things down."

Davis remarked, "Ah, yes. I hear Edwin Lee is a cousin of General Lee."

"Second cousins, I believe. At any rate, he and his wife arrived in Canada on January 24. It will be easy to transition him into Mr. Thompson's place as they have already been working on that contingency. Do I have your permission to implement transferring power from Mr. Thompson to the Brigadier?" Benjamin would also send orders for transferring Confederate funds in Canada to England. Those funds were intended for the re-constitution of the Confederacy at some later date.

"Do what needs to be done. Mr. Thompson is not my chief worry."

"We have many worries, for sure. However, we cannot afford to lose our crucial operation center in Canada."

"Yes, you're right, of course."

As Secretary Benjamin left the President's office, he muttered to himself, 'if only every problem we have were as easily resolved as Thompson.' A practical man, he had taken precautions when the tide appeared to turn against the South. Holding British citizenship, Judah had sent a share of his wealth to the United Kingdom months before. If the South should fall, he would flee there and resume his practice as a barrister. He could run his plantations in Louisiana remotely if need be, and if not, his land would lie fallow.

Were the Confederacy defeated, he anticipated many of the leading officials might well be tried for treason. He would not lack for Southern company as others would certainly flee. Judah wondered which of the more pragmatic officers in the government were insuring their financial futures and their lives in similar manner.

Thompson, for one, had let it slip that he had also transferred a substantial portion of his vast wealth to London. Judah did not know that Thompson had also sent for his wife Kate to join him in Montreal and to bring with her over $200,000 in stock certificates for cotton sold on the English market. The Thompsons would be on their way to England should the Confederacy fall.

Judah Benjamin, a non-practicing Sephardic Jew, a former U.S. Senator from Louisiana, and a lawyer before serving as Jefferson Davis's Secretary of State, was a shrewd man and a realist. His childhood had taught him that.

Judah's parents were living in St. Croix when he was born on August 11, 1811. His father, originally from London, was not successful there financially and moved the family to Fayetteville, N.C. where they had cousins. The Benjamins lived there for nine years but again financial difficulties dictated a relocation. Hoping for a better future, his father, Philip, moved part of the family to Charleston, S.C. This tolerant city was home to the largest Jewish community in the United States.   Judah and two siblings were left in Fayetteville for the next eighteen months in the custody of their cousins.   A student at the Fayetteville Academy, Judah's intellectual genius was recognized early on. After he moved to Charleston, Judah was expelled from the Jewish Reformation Congregation of which his father was a founder, due to Judah's failure to keep the Sabbath.

With the backing of a wealthy Charlestonian, the disgraced but brilliant Judah enrolled in Harvard at the age of fourteen. He left Harvard at sixteen without earning a degree and returned to Charleston for a brief stay with his family. He then moved to New Orleans where he worked as a law clerk to complete his legal education, was admitted to the bar, and studied French...a necessity for practicing law in Louisiana. Judah met and married Natalie Bauché de St. Martin, a Catholic from a wealthy Louisiana Creole family. The family was happy to transfer the unmanageable, head-strong Natalie into Judah's hands and he was ambitious enough to take her...along with a sizeable dowry. Their marriage, despite producing a daughter, was not a happy one. By the late 1840's she had moved to Paris with their only child. It was not until the 1850's that he managed to convince her to come to Washington and live with him there while he served in the Senate. That did not last, and she soon returned to Paris with their daughter. Benjamin was aware of the rumors that he was impotent and that was the reason his wife had left. Others, less charitable, suggested he was gay. With the outbreak of war, Judah returned to Louisiana until called to serve in Davis's Cabinet. In Richmond his wife's brother moved in with him. He ignored the slurs and inuendoes to concentrate on his role in the new government, his personal life remaining an enigma to others.

Despite the courage of its people, Judah knew the South could not survive on grit alone.   General Winfield Scott's great Anaconda Plan had finally squeezed shut the last open southern port when Wilmington fell the previous month. With no avenue for importing guns, cannons, ammunition, and the other necessities for conducting a war, things were beyond grim. For the people of the South with their fields barren, their livestock consumed by the armies of both sides, their men but for the very old and very young either dead, wounded, or still on the battlefield, their children starving, their dreams in dust, and with Sherman sweeping through the land with vengeance and fire destroying their very homes, many were consumed by misery and none were untouched by the horror they had lived through. The end of war would at least offer some path forward, just not the one they had fought for through four long and bloody years. Judah Benjamin was saddened and frustrated by the coming defeat, but life would go on.

JUDAH BENJAMIN'S MISSION FOR SARAH
Chapter 10

Sarah used the time while she waited for her next assignment to shop for another dress and a small trunk to hold her things. On the sixth of March, the message she had been expecting was delivered to her at the Spottswood. Sarah returned to Benjamin's office as ordered. When she arrived, she was kept waiting in the outer office. The clerk that manned the front office was so busy writing that he ignored her once he had told her to be seated. After an hour, a man she did not recognize left the Secretary's office and bustled out. The clerk looked up and motioned her to go in, before returning to his work.

Stressing the importance of the sealed document she would carry without disclosing what it contained, Benjamin handed it over along with the promised gold. "I suggest you carefully secret this paper on your person before you begin your trip north. Mr. Howell will meet you at your hotel early tomorrow morning. You might want to have breakfast and request a bit of food to take with you on your journey as the increased presence of enemy soldiers along your route may make progress slow. We also never know when one of our safe houses has been compromised. Howell is experienced in dealing with complications of this nature; therefore, I am trusting him to keep you safe and deal with unforeseen difficulties until he turns you over to the next escort. Good luck and be careful. I trust we will see you safely returned in less than three weeks."

"I will do my best, sir." Sarah left his office and began the walk back to the hotel.

She noticed a nervousness in those she encountered that had nothing to do with the spring storm that was beginning to blacken the sky. Wearing worn clothes that hung from underfed bodies, all looked worried and ill at ease. If the South were winning, surely there would not be such gloom on the faces she met. Sarah had no direct knowledge of the war other than the newspaper headlines she glanced at in the hotel lobby. She was content to leave those matters to men with gratitude that she did not have to endure the battles, cruelty, deaths, and gore that are the companions of war. Neither the politics of the day, nor the war had ever been more to her than a nuisance that interrupted life, separated her from her brothers and husband, and stole away the comforts and pleasures of daily life. Frederick's death from disease, not battle, and her missing brothers lay far more heavily on her heart than Rowan's absence.

With a foot in both camps due to being reared in the north and then moving south and marrying a southerner, she avoided conflicting sentiments by simply ignoring them, just as she tried not to worry about the fate of her brothers. All her life she had been taught that war and politics were the business of men. She was satisfied to leave them to it. Her sustaining hope was reunion with Eugene and Robert. With the gold she was earning, they would find a way to make far better lives for themselves than that of their parents. As long as she could believe in that future, Sarah was optimistic. It did not dawn on her to note the absence of Rowan in that dream.

Sarah rushed into the Spottswood Hotel just as heavy drops of rain began to pelt the streets turning them into a quagmire of mud that would soon be churned into ruts by carriages and wagons. Shaking the water from her skirt, she walked into the lobby and then to the stairs leading up. Upon reaching her room, the first order of business was a bit of sewing. Sarah gathered her sewing kit and her jacket. Taking a seat by the window, she used the light there to see what she was doing. She studied the pelisse carefully before ripping out the back lining. Sarah carefully flattened the vital document before re-stitching the seam. Unless she was subjected to a rigorous search it should be safe. Unless that document was discovered, there was nothing to implicate her in espionage. She would simply lie her way out of any trouble if she were stopped.

She left the hotel the following morning carrying the suggested extra food in her trunk. She hoped Howell had done the same. Howell took the trunk, and they walked to the depot where they boarded the train to Milford Station. Howell was jumpy throughout the entire journey to Milford and for once seemed to be in no mood to talk. Sarah watched him from under her eyelashes as he shifted from one position to another. The bench was hard, but his squirming was less about the bench, she suspected, than an inner unease. From time to time he would flex his jaw. Often, he turned to stare over his shoulder as though he felt he was being watched. Sarah was curious as to why he was so nervous when previously he had appeared sanguine to all dangers.

"Mr. Howell, is something bothering you? I cannot help but notice how ill at ease you are today."

His voice was just above a whisper when he replied. "The man sitting three rows back is Samuel Ruth, the owner of this railroad. He's been under suspicion as a Union spy and was arrested in February. The folks in Richmond kicked up a fuss and demanded he be released after only nine days in jail. I wasn't one of them protesting his innocence. I don't trust him, and I never have. Something about him just doesn't sit right with me."

Equally softly Sarah replied, "If the people in Richmond felt so strongly about his innocence, perhaps it's justified, and you are being unduly suspicious."

Howell shook his head, "I learned the hard way to trust my instinct. If I had done it sooner, I would not have been arrested twice. Both times, my guts told me to abort the mission, but I ignored it. I'm lucky to have escaped the rope after being arrested for transporting men from Maryland south to join the rebel army. I took their oath, but I've not stopped doing whatever I can. This trip with you is proof of that."

"Do you have any reason to suspect Mr. Ruth might be on to you?"

"I recognized him from the newspapers. My face was never in the papers, but he could have been informed about my activities by one of his handlers and told to watch me."

"I see." Sarah thought for a moment before adding. "Mr. Howell, perhaps we should take a different route north than the one you typically use."

"I've been thinking on that. I picked you up in Chaptico last time, and the route you took is the one we generally use. When we came back, I took you the mail route which I don't normally use, but it was arranged that we spend the night at Miss Floyd's home which is on the mail route. I don't want to use either one of those this time. I may have another option. I'll see what I can work out when we get to Milford. We have a horse and buggy waiting there, and there are some people in Milford I can trust. In the meantime, if we are stopped, we need to have a story ready. If you don't have any ideas, I do."

Sarah looked puzzled. She knew nothing about Maryland. That was his job wasn't it? "To be honest, I've had no reason to think up anything so far. That is up to you to handle."

"So, this is what I propose. If we are stopped, don't do the French bit. Yeah, you probably speak French, but I know that is a pretense you are using as I have heard you speak perfectly fine English. We're going to say you are my brother's widow and I am taking you home. I know the widow of Dr. John Huston who owned Poplar Hill Plantation on the Maryland side of the river. Sarah is a good woman and will take us in. The Stones are another option. That is more on our route than going east to Aquasco where I operated a tavern. If necessary, we will go to Aquasco and then turn back towards Washington. There are people in the Aquasco area who will vouch for me if need be. You let me do the talking if we're stopped by Yankees once we get to Maryland."

"Of course, whatever you think best. Is this going to add a lot of time to the trip?"

"Unfortunately, I suspect it will. I'm going to do some detouring so if anyone is following us, we can throw them off. We don't want to compromise any of the safe houses either."

"I suppose I should at least know your brother's name. By the way, I assume he's not married. It wouldn't do for him to have two wives."

"No, we won't be making him a bigamist." Howell chuckled before adding, "I'll just say he's my younger brother Adam. You don't need to say anything. I'll do the talking. If they start pushing you for answers, cry and become hysterical."

Now that Sarah knew why he was uncharacteristically

skittish, she was prepared to play whatever role would help them avoid arrest and continue on their way to Canada.

When they arrived at Milford Station, Howell walked to the livery stable to secure the horse and buggy that Benjamin had arranged for them. They encountered no problems leaving the station other than a long look from Samuel Ruth as they rode off. Howell noted the man's interest and decided he would veer from the normal route once they crossed the Potomac into Virginia.

Camden House, Port Royal, Virginia

The trip from Milford to Port Royal, Virginia, was uneventful, and there was no sign they were being followed. When they arrived in the town of 350 people, Howell drove on through and continued down river for another two miles. He made no comment about their destination other than to say he had a surprise for her. They turned left onto a well-maintained road that took them to a large plantation lying on the river. In the distance Sarah could see a grand Italianate mansion. As they neared, she gasped in surprise.

"You like it, do you?" Howell asked in amusement.

"That has to be the most beautiful home I have ever seen."

"It really is something. Wait to you see inside. It has the most modern of amenities: gas lighting, a coal furnace that sends heat through wooden ducts to every room, and using cool air from the basement the ducts cool the house in summer. It even has bathrooms with toilets and hot and cold water. In the basement, there's a huge wine cellar and a kitchen. The basement walls and floors are brick to protect against fires."

Charles Pratt, Earl of Camden

"The owners must be very wealthy."

"Very. The wealth originated in England. When they came here, they bought hundreds of acres of fertile farmland on the banks of the river and built a wood-frame house. This is one of the largest plantations around these parts. When the current owner, William Pratt, inherited the plantation and married his wife Eliza in 1858, she insisted on something nicer. Mr. Pratt had the original house torn down and a Philadelphia architect designed the one that now stands on the old site. It's called Camden House as Mr. Pratt's ancestor was Charles Pratt, the Earl of Camden."

Sarah studied the house. Balustrades surrounded the roofs of the first-floor porches, as well as, a semi-circular solarium on the left, and second-floor balconies. Floor to ceiling windows with rounded tops on both levels were topped with elaborate carved cornices. The second-floor eaves were supported by ornate brackets. A broad porch wrapped the front of the house and extended around the sides. Sarah puzzled, "It looks like the design is off somehow?"

"There used to be a tower on the roof and all they've done is patch the spot temporarily. In '62 a Yankee gunboat fired bullets at the house nearly killing Mrs. Pratt and their ailing newborn baby as she was putting the infant in bed to sleep. Had she not been leaning over they would have both been killed. You can still see where the bullet hit the wall above her head. Once the Yankees had the range, they fired five-inch shrapnel filled cannons balls until they blew the tower to smithereens."

"Why would they do that?" Sarah cried.

"A tower on the house was an ideal lookout point for the Confederates to monitor Yankee boats on the river, so they destroyed it."

"How is it we get to stay here?"

"After that cannon ball, you might say they are even more ardent Confederates. They also are friends of Secretary Benjamin. He has arranged for me to use it for special couriers. I guess that makes you one."

A uniformed servant met them at the end of the drive. He held out his hand to take the horse's bridle. "Welcome, Mr. Howell. We been awaitin' for y'all."

"Hey, Rastus. You doing well?"

"Yassuh, doin' fine. I gwine take this here hoss and buggy. I git yo' stuff and take'em on in for y'all. The massah and mistress be waiting' for y'all inside."

Howell climbed down from the buggy and walked to the other side to assist Sarah in alighting. Taking her elbow, he escorted her to the front porch.

The front door opened, and a neatly dressed negress smiled in welcome. "Please come in. The Pratts are waiting for you in the sunroom. They were just having a glass of before-supper sherry. I will bring you a glass as soon as you get settled."

"Thank you, Emiline."

Sarah gazed around the foyer in awe. With the coming of evening, a tri-globed gasolier lit the entry. Sarah noted the seemingly unsupported stairway that swirled up to the next level. Underfoot, a thick Turkish carpet muted their footsteps. As they walked down the hall to the solarium, she turned her head from side to side trying to take it all in. She had never dreamed of entering such a palatial home, much less spending the night in one.

When they entered the solarium, William Pratt immediately rose, making a slight bow in Sarah's direction. "Ah, you must be the new courier Judah told me to expect. He failed to tell me what a lovely one he is sending on errands now. Mrs. Slater, I believe, I'm William Pratt and this is my wife, Eliza."

Entry Hall, Camden House

Turning to Howell, he slapped him on the shoulder, "I see you are still eluding the Yankees, Gus."

"I'm doing my best, sir. I appreciate your hospitality for the night. It's good to be able to stay in such delightful accommodations."

"Don't mention it. I'm glad to do what I can for the cause. Please, you two have a seat. We are just having a bit of sherry. Emiline will be bringing you both a glass shortly."

The woman was there almost before the words left his mouth. Pratt wasted no time in quizzing Howell about the latest news of battles and conditions in Richmond. While the men talked war, Eliza tried to draw Sarah out by asking her about herself. When

Sarah's answers were brief and noncommittal, Eliza gave up...assuming as a covert operative, the beautiful woman was perforce secretive. Eliza switched to talking about the house of which she was passionately proud.

When supper was announced, the Pratts led them to the formal dining room. Set with heavy silver, gold edged china, and fragile crystal, the table glistened under the gas-lit chandelier. The Pratts seemed to have avoided many of the culinary deprivations of the war. Over supper, William Pratt explained that they were fortunate their fields and gardens provided generously enough they could give to the army and still have enough left for their own needs. From the river, they gathered an abundance of fish and the surrounded woodland afforded game to supplement their domestic animals. Like other southern households there was no sugar, however plantation beehives provided ample honey.

Parlor, Camden House

After supper, they adjourned to the parlor that was furnished with velvet upholstered Victorian Rococo furniture, windows framed by heavy tasseled draperies topped by gilded pelmets, oil portraits of various Pratt family members, and a marble fireplace. In one corner was a rosewood piano. Walking over to the piano, Sarah hungrily slid her fingers over the satin-smooth wood.

"Do you play, Mrs. Slater?" Eliza asked.

"I do. If you would like, I am happy to play for you."

"We would be delighted," William answered for his wife.

Sarah sat at the piano and began to play songs that she loved and for which she needed no sheet music. After the third song, she began to sing. Her audience listened with rapt attention until she stopped and quietly closed the lid.

"My word, Mrs. Slater. You could easily appear professionally. What a gift you have. That piano would applaud you if it could after my poor attempts to play it," Eliza remarked with a smile.

When goodnights were said, Emiline appeared to lead Sarah to her room on the second floor. When Sarah entered the room, she paused for a moment to gape before recovering herself. She did not want the servant to know how awed she was by the luxurious room. Emiline did not notice her expression as she was busy pointing out Sarah's nightgown on the turned down bed, the armoire that now held the contents of her trunk, the control for the gas light, and the water pitcher and glass that sat on a tray atop a vanity by the window. Opening the door to the left of the bed, she beckoned Sarah to enter the bathroom. Inside Sarah found a large tub, sink, and a flush toilet. Emiline showed her the fresh towels and toiletries and asked if she needed anything more. Sarah shook her head and thanked the woman.

When the maid had left, Sarah spread her arms and turned in a circle to admire the room. The huge bed was covered with a canopy draped in the same fabric as that at the windows where the drapes were drawn closed for the night. The rug underfoot was as plush as the ones downstairs. A dainty loveseat, two chairs, and a small table were placed near the fireplace. Two ornate grillwork panels poured warm air into the room. Sarah wasted no time in discarding her clothes and running water into the tub. Picking up the bottles on the shelf by the tub, she selected perfumed bath salts and sifted them into the water. Soon she was immersed to her neck in steaming water that smelled of roses. She could have spent the night in the tub, but the water was beginning to cool, and she had been warned they would be leaving at first light. She needed to get some sleep.

Sarah toweled herself dry, pulled on the nightgown that suddenly looked cheap despite her best effort to enhance it with tucking and lace. Sliding her hands down her curvaceous body, she cursed herself for settling for a husband like the hapless Rowan when Eliza had married someone like William Pratt. Jealousy flared in her breast. Sarah shrugged her shoulders in resignation; for the moment she was doing the best she could. But, as she drifted off to sleep in the nicest bed that had ever held her, she swore she would find a better future. If a woman like the moderately attractive Eliza could have this kind of life, why couldn't she…wasn't she far more beautiful, clever, and talented?

CROSSING RIVERS
Chapter 11

A knock on the door was immediately followed by the slight squeal of a hinge as the door to her bedroom opened. Drowsily, Sarah roused from a deep sleep to see Emiline walk across the room and draw the drapes. The dim light of dawn poured into the room. It was with some chagrin that Sarah decided the life of a courier did not involve luxuriating in bed come morning.

Emiline announced, "I have you a pot of what passes for coffee nowadays and a hot ham biscuit for your breakfast. Mr. Pratt and Mr. Howell are both up and dressed. They say you need to be ready to leave in thirty minutes."

Sarah swung her legs over the side of the bed. "Thank you, Emiline. I'll not waste time."

Emiline nodded and left the room. Sarah used the bathroom and washed her face. She looked longingly at the tub, but knew another bath was a vain dream. She returned to the bedroom where she hurriedly donned her clothing, drank the ersatz coffee, ate the ham biscuit, and then stowed her nightgown and hairbrush in her small trunk before arranging the hat and veil on her head. She looked around the lovely room one last time, before leaving to join the waiting men.

Rastus was standing beside their buggy holding the bridle as he waited for Sarah to descend the front steps. William Pratt assisted her to climb in the buggy while Howell took his seat and picked up the reins. Sarah barely had time to thank Pratt before Howell was slapping the reins. She looked back at the house as they drove down the drive. With the ground covered in a deep frost, it seemed to float like a mirage in the early morning light.

Port Royal, Virginia

They were first in line for the Port Royal ferry across the Rappahannock. When they pulled the buggy on board followed by several pedestrians, the ferryman maneuvered the raft away from the pier. On the open river, a stiff wind lifted Sarah's veil to momentarily expose her face. She glanced around to see if anyone had noticed as she repositioned it to hide her features. Removing one of the pins that secured her hair, she used it to hold the veil in place as the bitterly cold wind continued to tug at it. Crossing her arms, she clutched her shawl to her chest to conserve body heat. She was relieved when they reached the opposite shore and moved into the lee of land.

Since they were still in Virginia until they crossed the Potomac, Howell made good time crossing the peninsula that lay between the Rappahannock and the Potomac Rivers despite the light snow that began falling. By the time they reached Mathias point and Lt. Cawood's Confederate Signal Camp, an inch of snow covered the ground.

Howell remarked to Sarah, "I think it's best we don't try to cross the river until first thing in the morning. My contact here, James Wiltshire, will be rowing us over to the Maryland shore. He has arranged for someone to meet us on the other side with a horse and buggy for the remainder of the trip to Washington. Mr. Wiltshire will meet us at the camp in the morning unless the weather gets worse. Unfortunately, you're not going to find the local accommodations nearly as nice as what you had last night. Lt. Cawood has an arrangement with the Brown family not far from here. They're a farm family that lets people stay from time to time to bring in a little money. You will find they're hospitable and the place is clean."

Ten minutes later they drove into a small farmyard delineated by a split rail fence. An unpainted farmhouse was bracketed by two oak trees, the limbs bare and limned with snow. To the right of the house was a barn, chicken coop, and a shed. It was a far cry from the Italianate mansion where they had spent the previous night. Wiping her hands on her apron, then smoothing her graying hair back into the knot at the back of her head, Mrs. Brown stood on the porch waiting for them as they descended from the buggy.

A cheery smile lit her work-worn features, "Y'all come on in out of the cold now, Mr. Howell, and set yourselves down by the fire to warm up. Soon as Pa comes in, we'll eat us some vittles. He's down at the pen slopping what hogs the army saw fit to leave us."

Howell spoke up, "Thank you, Mrs. Brown. It will take me a minute to stable the horse and put the buggy in the shed. I'll be right back. The lady with me is Mrs. Slater."

"That's fine. You go on and do what you need to do with your horse while I settle the lady by the fire." Mrs. Brown turned to Sarah, "Come on in dear. It's too cold to stand around out here."

Sarah followed the woman into the room that served as kitchen, dining room, and sitting room. A hot fire blazed in the fireplace, where a black iron kettle was swung off to the side for cooking slowly over the coals. The aroma of stewing meat assailed Sarah's nostrils to remind her she had eaten little all day. Her stomach rumbled in anticipation.

Mrs. Brown laughed, "I don't think that man's fed you much. Why don't I give you a piece of cornbread soaked in clabber while we wait for the men? I know it ain't much, but that'll tide you over just fine."

"Thank you, ma'am. I am famished."

While Mrs. Brown bustled about the kitchen, Sarah warmed her hands by the fire after she had eaten the cornbread. Her feet were nearly frozen, too. Slipping out of footwear that was far too dainty for the weather, Sarah edged her feet closer to the warm blaze. Leather gloves, warm woolen socks, and lace up shoes like Howell wore were far more practical than her mittens, stockings, and slippers. When Howell returned from settling the horse, he stamped his feet on the porch before entering the kitchen. Mrs. Brown set a bowl of warm water and a towel on the chest by the door so they could wash their hands. Sarah and Howell had just dried off, when Mr. Brown came in. His face was ruddy with cold. Using the same towel and water, he washed up too after greeting Howell and nodding to Sarah.

Their ablutions done, the three of them joined Mrs. Brown at the table where she had set steaming bowls of stew. In the center of the table was a platter of cornbread. She poured water into their four glasses, before taking her seat. After Mr. Brown said grace, Sarah tried the stew that smelled so good. Carrots, potatoes, dried tomatoes, and onions had cooked tender along with dried sausage making for a savory dish. Forcing herself, not to gulp it down, Sarah ate it all. When Mrs. Brown ladled seconds for everyone, Sarah did not decline.

Mrs. Brown commented, "Sad to say, these are the last of the carrots and potatoes in the root cellar. We will have to wait for summer to enjoy them again."

Her husband added, "Looks like pickings are going to be mighty scarce around here for a while except for what we are lucky enough to buy. We appreciate your visits, Mr. Howell, and the other folks Lieutenant Cawood sends, as they bring us payment in gold coin we can use to buy any extras our neighbors may have. The confederate paper money we have is neigh onto worthless. Nobody wants it anymore. If this war don't get over soon so we can get back to normal life, I don't know what folks are going to do."

Howell replied, "Well, I am sure the Lieutenant is as grateful for your help as I am. Repaying you for housing and feeding us is the least we can do."

Following supper, Sarah helped wash the dishes. Afterwards, Mrs. Brown banked the fire in the fireplace after shoveling some of the hot coals into a warming pan for her bed. She apologized for the sleeping arrangements as she asked Sarah to help her make pallets for her and Howell to sleep on. The woman strung a blanket down the center of the kitchen with a pallet for Sarah on one side and one for Howell on the other. The men came in from the porch where they had gone to smoke their pipes. Wasting no time, the Browns took their warming pan into the small room off the kitchen.

Howell chuckled, "Like I said, this is a little different from last night. Take the pallet you want, and I'll take the other...not that it makes much difference."

Sarah shrugged her shoulders and stepped behind the blanket to the pallet nearest the fireplace. It was growing chilly with the fire banked, so she kept her clothes on as she laid down and pulled the quilts over her. Going to sleep was soon to be problematic. No sooner than Sarah had begun to feel drowsy than a stentorian snore emerged from the other side of the dividing blanket that was echoed by one from the Brown's bedroom. Listening to the creaking of wood as the cabin cooled and the noise of owls and other birds of the night to take her mind off the snores, she eventually fell into restless slumber. It was with relief when morning came, and they could thank the Browns and be on their way.

Howell noticed Sarah's grim mood. "Are you feeling ill or something?"

Sarah snapped, "Annoyed is a more apt term. I could barely sleep for the racket you made. Between you and Mr. Brown, I don't know who snored worse."

Choosing not to answer, Howell began to whistle tunelessly. That, too, grated on Sarah's nerves, until she finally exploded. "Could you just be quiet?"

"You sure are a grumpy nellie this morning, Mrs. Slater."

Her reply was a terse, "Thank you, Mr. Howell."

Gus Howell did not like the looks of the grey low-hanging clouds. With snow on the ground, more snow or sleet would make their trip even more difficult. He would be glad to reach Maryland and turn Sarah over to Fowle as he had another woman to escort back to Richmond.

Lieutenant Cawood and James Wiltshire were waiting for them when they arrived at the signal camp. Wiltshire led them to the signal corps pier where the camp's boat was tied up. Next to it was a smaller boat that Wiltshire had procured to row them across the Potomac. Sarah looked at the small boat and the white caps on the river. The cold, dismal weather that chilled to the bone was bad enough, but the thought of being on the river in a small boat that could be capsized by waves filled her with mortal alarm. Even if she could swim, there was no surviving in water that cold.

Biting her lip, she controlled the urge to stutter. "Surely, you don't mean to attempt the river crossing now, Mr. Wiltshire?"

"I'm afraid we must, ma'am. It looks like the weather is going to get worse. We might as well cross while we can. It's not as bad as it looks. I've crossed when it was a lot rougher."

"Well, I haven't!" Sarah yelled.

Wiltshire calmly replied, "No, ma'am. I suspect not. You are going to be just fine. I don't risk my neck when I think it is too dangerous to cross. You need to trust me to know what I'm doing."

Sarah muttered under her breath, "What choice do you idiot men give me?"

Howell hid his grin. He knew Mrs. Slater was mad as hell even though he could not hear what she mumbled. When he offered to help her into the boat, she jerked her elbow out of his hand and nearly tumbled overboard before she could right herself. Saying nothing, the two men took their seats. Each of them grabbed an oar and pushed the boat from shore.

Out of the lee of the shore, the waves were higher, occasionally splashing water into the boat. Sarah's grip on the gunnels was so tight she could not be bothered to wring out the hem of her skirt. By the time they had crossed the Potomac to Swan Point, Sarah was exhausted from nervous tension. She was stiff and awkward when she tried to climb out of the boat. Wordlessly, Howell extended his hand and helped her out. He had not much cared for the crossing either. Standing under the shelter of a grove of pines, a man emerged leading two horses and a buggy. Sarah recognized James Fowle, the man that had met her in Port Tobacco on her previous trip.

Sarah climbed into the buggy and pulled the half of the lap robe over her legs and tucked it in under her arms. Howell climbed in beside her and took his half of the robe to cover his own legs. Slapping the reins on the back of a horse that acted as though it had more sense than men to be out in such miserable weather, the buggy moved off at a balky pace. Riding beside the buggy, Fowle leaned over to tell Howell he thought they should avoid Port Tobacco, as there was too much Yankee presence in the town to risk going to Rose Hill to spend the night.

Howell thought for a moment, before asking, "Do you think the Stone house, Haberdeventure, is safe?"

"It should be as it's far enough out. I'll ride ahead and check it out when we get closer. If it looks risky, we'll figure out something else. If you reach over your shoulder, Gus, you'll find a bundle with some cornbread and sweet potatoes. If you're hungry, it won't matter if it's cold."

"I could eat a raw bear: claws, hide and all." Howell laughed his good mood restored.

Sarah was hungry, too. She reminded herself not to be so waspish. These men were enduring cold, hunger, and hardship...not to mention risking their lives to get her to her destination. "That sounds wonderful, Mr. Fowle. While I'm not sure I could eat a bear, cornbread and sweet potatoes will do just fine."

Fowle laughed before saying, "Ma made them. I already ate mine so what's left is for the two of you."

Howell reached behind the seat to grab the package containing food. With something in their stomachs, the cold would not be so unbearable. Soon, both Sarah and Howell were eating the food Fowle's mother had packed for them. When they were finished, not even a crumb remained inside the oiled paper.

"Lord, the world suddenly looks a lot brighter to me." Howell remarked.

Sarah felt genuine contrition when she responded, "To me, as well. Please, excuse my foul temper earlier. I do appreciate all you are risking by helping me get to Canada even if I did not show it earlier."

"Think nothing of it. This weather makes the best of us miserable, but at least we can be grateful we haven't run into a patrol."

The moment the words left his mouth, two Yankee soldiers

rode into the road and faced their way, pistols leveled. The one on the left ordered them to halt as they rode closer. Both Howell and Fowle raised their hands in the air.

The soldier on the right barked, "You put your hands up, too, ma'am."

Feeling the dig of Howell's elbow in her ribs, Sarah began to cry piteously.

"Mister, my sister-in-law is in mourning as you can see. We just got word my brother, a Union soldier like you men, was killed down in Petersburg. This other man here is Preacher Fowle's son. The preacher has arranged a graveside service and we're just trying to get there." While Howell responded, Sarah raised her sobs to a hysterical pitch.

Union Camp, photo Mathew Brady

Sarah moaned, "Oh, my Adam, my poor Adam."

The man glanced from her back to Howell, "I'm sorry for your troubles, but I still need to see some papers."

Howell and Fowle both handed over theirs to the man on the left. He looked them over and handed them back. "Now, let me see yours, ma'am."

Sarah silently swore. Her papers were made out for Nettie Slater of Canada since she was traveling as a citizen of that country. They would not explain her presence at a funeral in Maryland for a fictitious husband whose name she did not carry. She nodded her head at the soldier as she began pawing frantically in her valise, crying louder all the time.

Taking pity, the man said, "It's alright, ma'am. I'm sorry for your loss. You folks go on to the funeral."

When they were out of earshot, both Howell and Fowle began to laugh.

"What's so funny?" Sarah demanded. "I was scared to death we were going to be arrested."

Howell said, "I told you to cry and act hysterical, but I never dreamed you were capable of that kind of performance. To tell you the truth, I was about ready to cry for dear brother Adam myself...trouble is, I don't have a brother Adam."

"You should go on the stage, Mrs. Slater," Fowle added.

Even as Sarah joined them in the hilarity, she decided if she made another trip, she would have more than one set of false papers to explain where she was going.

AT MARY'S HOUSE
Chapter 12

It was nightfall when they arrived at Haberdeventure, the former home of a Revolutionary soldier and one of the 57 signatories of the Declaration of Independence, Thomas Stone. Stone had died in 1787, but the property was still owned by his direct descendants. The brick main house was fronted by a porch that stretched its entire façade, while both sides were flanked by additions built to house his expanded family…necessitated when his father died leaving five younger brothers and sisters to move in with him, his wife, and two daughters.

Sarah and the two men were exhausted, hungry, and close to frost bitten when they arrived at Haberdeventure. To add to their misery, a cold sleet had begun to fall. They were still over twenty-five miles from Washington and Fowle worried a delay would put Sarah behind schedule to make connections there. It was Fowle's job to get her to Washington as Howell would leave in the morning for another assignment.

When they drove up, a Negro lad of early teen years darted from behind the house to take the horses and buggy. Howell thanked him, as he helped Sarah to the ground and then grabbed her trunk.

Howell escorted Sarah, followed by James Fowle, to the front door. By the time they reached it, the door swung open. A tall, handsome woman of perhaps forty years of age, smiled in welcome.

Haberdeventure, near Port Tobacco, Maryland

"James, we have been expecting you but with such dreadful weather, we were unsure you would make it. Please, come in. You must all be near frozen."

Fowle introduced his two companions, as the woman…who introduced herself as Margaret Stone…led them inside. From the foyer, they followed her into the parlor, striking for its blue-painted, paneled and wainscoted walls. Wine-hued drapery and upholstery softened the appearance of the paneling and dark wood floor. Sarah noted a mahogany piano in the corner, thinking at least she could repay the Stones' hospitality with music. They settled themselves before the fire, Sarah on the small sofa and the two men on chairs, while Margaret Stone pulled a bell cord that hung by the fireplace. In short order, a Negress of short stature and broad girth arrived at the door where she paused to await orders.

"Jemma, would you bring our guests some mulled wine please and a plate of your tea cakes."

The servant departed to reappear moments later with a tray bearing four glasses, and a plate of cookies. After passing the refreshments around, she placed the plate on a side table should anyone want more. Following her departure with the empty tray, Margaret said, "I suspect travel tomorrow will be difficult if the sleet freezes on top of the snow we've already had. I am sure you are eager to be on your way in the morning, but if it is dangerous, you must stay here until it's safe to travel."

Howell responded, "As you say, haste is necessary, but if it's treacherous in the morning, it would be remiss of us to risk our necks or the horses by leaving precipitously. We'll try not to inconvenience you any longer than need be, however, as we are conscious of the urgency of our missions."

Howell thought about the woman he was supposed to meet at Merrywood in the morning to escort to Richmond. The daring Loretta Velazquez worked as a double agent, both for Richmond and for Colonel Lafayette Baker, chief detective for the Union and noted spymaster whom she had duped into hiring her. The cold-eyed and abrupt Baker did not know the name of the Confederate woman he was after and charged Loretta with finding her. He explained the 'she-devil' he was seeking was known to have made trips in 1864 to both Ohio and Canada carrying money to fund an attempted rescue of Confederate soldiers imprisoned on Johnson's Island in Lake Erie. Loretta told Baker she thought she knew the woman that he sought, and circuitously had a photograph of another woman delivered to him and identified as that spy. Loretta, already a Confederate spy, remained an asset to Richmond from 1864 to 1865 for the information she picked up in Washington while acting as a double agent. Howell was amused by her bravado when she told him on a previous trip that Baker had essentially hired her to find herself.

Interrupting Howell's train of thought, Margaret continued,

"You folks are no inconvenience, so rest your mind on that score. In the country as we are, and with things in turmoil due to the war, it is good to have guests to give us news of the outside world. Mr. Stone will return shortly, and I'm sure he will exhaust your patience with his questions. We are most curious as to what is happening in Richmond. The newspapers we receive are all proclaiming the end of the war is near. But, all of that can wait.

Loretta Janetta Velasquez

"Supper will be in an hour or so. In the interim, I have two guest rooms prepared for you upstairs. I will ask you gentlemen to share one, and Mrs. Slater the other. After you have warmed up and finished your refreshments, I will show you to your rooms. Jemma has a fire going in the fireplaces so the chill should be off the rooms by then. There are also pitchers of water and towels to freshen up."

Sarah was relieved to reach her room and find it not only warm near the fire, but furnished with carved ebony furniture, a tall armoire, flamboyantly embroidered yellow bedcoverings and matching drapes at the dormer window, a bed that looked soft and inviting, and a braided rug underfoot. A rocking chair and a small table bearing an unlit candle sat near the fireplace. With Fowle destined to endure Howell's snoring during the coming night, she should at least get more sleep than on the pallet in the Brown's kitchen.

Sarah removed her hat with the heavy black veil and her wrinkled mourning dress. She stared at the dress with distaste. She was sick of the drab widow's weeds she was per force wearing while traveling and wanted to look young and appealing…not for others, but for her own satisfaction. The water Sarah poured in the basin was cold, but she bathed as best she could, before pulling on the frock she had made when first staying with the Campbells. The long sleeves, high neckline with white lace collar, and woolen fabric would be warm. Haberdeventure did not have the centralized heating of Camden House and even with fireplaces roaring, the outer edges of the rooms were cold. She was also aware the yellow fabric was flattering to her complexion and the dress was cut to mold to her figure.

Sarah heard the door to the room the men were sharing open and close, followed by their footsteps as they descended the stairs. Taking a last look in the mirror of the armoire door where she had hung her black dress, Sarah closed the armoire and left her own room to join the others for dinner.

Sarah noted the looks of admiration turned her way by both Gus Howell and the shyer James Fowle as she descended the stairs. She hoped the admiration would not spur Howell to renew his annoying flirtation. She much preferred his more professional behavior of the last few days. She was not worried about Fowle pushing his attentions on her as he was much too reserved. She did not have long to think about trivia, as over dinner the Stones began a vigorous discussion of the war that had them all involved and offering a variety of perspectives.

Following dinner, Sarah played the piano and sang. Margaret, who's alto voice was quite good but no match for Sarah's soprano, joined her. During the second song, *Lorena*, Fowle came to stand by Margaret and joined his tenor voice to theirs. Mr. Stone and Howell were an enthusiastic audience. All were reluctant for the evening to come to an end, but morning and departure would come early.

Sarah awakened in the morning when a servant came in to stir the coals in the fireplace and add more wood. She waited until the logs took hold and began to warm the room before throwing back the covers and walking to the window. The world outside glistened in the morning light as the sun lit up granules of the frozen sleet that now covered the snow. She was not sorry when Fowle informed her over breakfast that they would be waiting another day in hopes it would be less treacherous. Howell had left before she came down. Fowle explained that Howell felt he had no choice but to risk going since he would be on horseback and not dealing with both horse and buggy.

Sarah grinned before remarking, "I trust you will sleep better tonight than last night."

Sarah could not help laughing when Fowle said, "I wish someone had told me Howell could saw logs that way. I would have slept in the stable with the horses if I had known."

After breakfast with the Stones, Margaret invited Sarah to join her in the parlor. They spent much of the day reading by the fireplace. Margaret had given Sarah *The Newcomes* by Thackeray to read. She said that Sarah could take it with her when she left as she would not have time to finish it before leaving the following morning since by late afternoon the coating of ice had begun to melt.

Surratt Boardinghouse, Washington, D.C.,
courtesy the Surratt Museum

Fowle and Sarah left early the next morning. The sun of the previous day and temperatures above freezing during the night had melted the ice and most of the snow. Although the roads were muddy and increasingly rutted as they went through towns along the way, they were still in Washington by 8:00 P.M. on Sunday, March 12. Sarah was to spend the night in the Surratt boarding house while Fowle planned to stay with a friend who would take him in for the night.

Mary Surratt met Sarah at the door and explained that because all the rented rooms were occupied one of the boarders had agreed to let her use his. Louis Wiechmann was happy to give up his room to the beautiful widow and move in with John Surratt for the night. Wiechman glanced back over his shoulder in admiration before taking Sarah's small trunk up to his room while Mary led Sarah to the kitchen.

Following a quick supper of cold leftovers, the devoutly religious Mrs. Surratt asked Sarah to join her in the parlor for her nightly reading of the Bible. Mary's daughter Anne joined them. Mary's son John, who had gone out earlier, had not yet returned. Following the reading and prayer, they said their rosaries. As Sarah did not have her rosary with her, Mary loaned her an extra one she had in a drawer of the desk that sat by the window. The evening was a good one for Sarah as it had been a long time since she had practiced her Catholic faith, and she had missed it.

After they said goodnight and went to their rooms, Sarah was ready to crawl in bed. In the room beside hers, she could hear the low rumble of voices...three she identified as John Surratt, Louis Wiechmann, and George Atzerodt; the fourth voice she did not recognize...nor could she understand the low-pitched rumble of their voices. Turning onto her side away from the sounds from the adjacent room, she soon drifted off.

While she slept, Wiechmann wasted no time in learning all he could about the fascinating Mrs. Slater. Surratt told him that although she was from North Carolina, she was French and acting as a courier for the Confederacy. But the men, including John Wilkes Booth…the voice Sarah could not identify, had more important things to talk about than Sarah. Surratt, Atzerodt, and Booth were plotting to kidnap President Lincoln on Friday, March 17, when he was scheduled to go to Campbell Hospital, the President's summer residence, on the outskirts of Washington to see a performance of "Still Waters Run Deep." Wiechmann was all ears as he listened to what the men were plotting. The others were unaware that Wiechmann was a bit of a blabbermouth having already told a fellow clerk in the office where he worked that Confederates were staying at the Surratt boarding house.

John Surratt and Sarah left the following morning, March 13, to take the train to New York. It was not until she unpacked her trunk in New York that she realized she had left a pair of slippers at the Surratt boarding house. Sarah was provoked as the dainty slippers were favorites of hers. She reminded herself to be sure to retrieve the slippers when she went back through Washington. Surratt was already on his way back to Washington. He had explained she would be on her own the remainder of the trip, as he was planning something important that required his immediate return to Washington. He added that he would probably be the one assigned to meet her in New York when she traveled back from Canada. He did not tell her why he was in such a rush, and she did not care enough to ask.

Left in New York, Sarah was completely on her own. In some

ways, she considered it safer. She knew the route to take, the procedure at the Canadian border, where to go in Montreal, and with papers declaring her a Canadian citizen, she expected no problems she could not handle.

Before leaving, Sarah paid her mother a brief visit, treated her to dinner, and gave her another twenty-dollar gold piece. Although Antoinette's eyes lit up at the bright gold coin, she only nodded her gratitude. Sarah left still hungry for some indication her mother loved her.

On Saint Patrick's Day, Friday, March 17, she was back in Montreal and delivered her documents to Thompson and Edwin Lee. They warned her to expect departure back to Richmond as soon as they could prepare the necessary responses to the documents she had brought and arrange for an escort to meet her in New York.

For the next three days, Sarah enjoyed the time relaxing and seeing the sights of Montreal. It was a pleasure to speak the French language she had grown up with as she dined in the city's restaurants and explored the small shops selling things that made her drool. After four years in the war-torn and deprived South, it was a delight to have good food, real coffee, and to see shops filled with all kinds of merchandise.

Even though she reminded herself to be prudent with her gold coins, Sarah could not resist a particularly beautiful yellow cashmere shawl and a pearl encrusted pair of tortoise shell hair combs that she saw in one of the shop windows. Walking into the boutique, she greeted the woman behind the counter and asked about the items in the window. When Sarah felt the softness of the shawl and saw how nice the combs looked in her hair, she knew she had to have them. Ten minutes later, having bargained with the woman for a lower price, Sarah left with the combs and shawl neatly wrapped in a package. In another shop, she found a black woolen cape with a hood and fleece lined low boots. She justified their purchase as Montreal was cold enough that the St. Lawrence River was frozen solid and the wind from the river cut through her like a knife. Furthermore, walking about the city would be far more comfortable with something warm to wear. She donned both shoes and cape before she exited the shop. She hated that her purse was lighter, but if they continued using her services as a courier, she could easily replace what she had spent.

On the morning of the 21st, she left Montreal with documents to deliver to Judah Benjamin and ten twenty-dollar gold coins in payment for her services. She hefted her purse with satisfaction as she left Lee's office. While she did not like the rigors of winter travel, she hoped Benjamin would send her to Montreal for another mission.

Two days earlier, Brigadier General Lee had written a telegram to John Surratt to meet Sarah's train in New York on the 23rd. Sarah hoped he would not keep her waiting as he had the last time he met her in New York.

THE AMERICAN IDOL
Chapter 13

When Sarah alit from the train in New York, she spotted John Surratt on the platform. Standing beside him was another man possessed of Byronic good looks…slim, elegant, curly dark locks falling on his forehead, well-dressed. She found herself pausing in mid-stride to momentarily stare. As she approached, Sarah noticed she was not the only woman casting admiring glances his way.   Sarah schooled herself not to gape, when Surratt introduced the man as the famous actor, John Wilkes Booth. Although she had never seen him perform, his fame…and that of his family…was legendary.

Booth took her hand and bent over to kiss it as though she were royalty. "Ah, the beauteous widow, Mrs. Slater. John told me you are lovely, but his description does not begin to do justice to the reality."

He tucked her hand in his elbow as John scurried off like a lackey to fetch Sarah's trunk. She was not sure she liked Booth's arrogant assumption of familiarity or how he treated his friend as nothing more than a servant. Even so, Sarah was flattered by the attention of one of America's idols. He maintained an effortless stream of words that made her feel important and admired. By the time John Surratt returned with her trunk balanced on his shoulder, Sarah was in danger of being smitten. Jealousy flared in Surratt's eyes as he noticed the possessive way Booth held Sarah's hand on his arm.

Despite his initial excitement at the invitation, Surratt

suddenly resented that Booth had made arrangements for them to dine together at the renowned Delmonico's Restaurant on William Street. Booth was in his element there, whereas Surratt realized he would look like an untutored bumpkin next to the suave actor. While John Surratt hailed a passing taxi to take Sarah to her hotel, Booth again kissed her hand saying he looked forward to the pleasure of seeing her at dinner.

Rooms had been booked for them at the Metropolitan Hotel on the corner of Broadway and Prince Street. When they drove up to the grand Roman-Palazzo style hotel, Sarah was impressed. Elegant shops occupied the ground floor of the building, tempting Sarah with the beautiful displays. The interior was even more impressive with the largest plate glass mirrors in the country, furnishings imported from Europe, heavy draperies at the corniced windows, plush rugs on the marble floors, large palms dotted about the lobby, and copious gilding.

Metropolitan Hotel, New York, N.Y.

With business down, Sarah and John Surratt were given a hearty welcome. Although the hotel could hold six hundred guests, the toll of war had left many rooms empty. A porter carried her trunk as he escorted Sarah to her room, describing the features of the hotel as he walked. He described Niblo Garden, a three hundred seat theater in the basement where guests could attend nightly musicals. He bragged that Mary Todd Lincoln, as well as her maid, used the hotel whenever she visited New York. He glanced at Sarah, before adding, "Unlike other hotels, we allow Negro servants to stay with their masters." When they reached her room, he unlocked the door and placed her trunk on the floor. Walking to the desk by the window, he picked up a menu explaining that the hotel operated on the American Plan. Noting the puzzled look on her face, he explained that all three meals a day were provided along with the room.

As the porter finished with his introduction to the hotel, Sarah thanked him before he left. Looking around the room, Sarah noted the steam heat and the luxury of a private bathroom with hot and cold water. She stood in a quandary for a moment. Should she bathe and relax before dressing for dinner, or should she hurry down to explore the shops while she had the chance and spend less time bathing and dressing? The lure of the shops, designed to seduce women, was too magnetic too ignore.

Sarah grabbed her purse and hurried down to the lobby and out to the street. Turning right she explored the luxurious shops on that side, then reversed to check the ones on the left side of the hotel. One seemed to draw her attention more than the others. Opening the door to the sound of a bell merrily tinkling overhead, Sarah was immediately welcomed by a mustachioed clerk. He inquired if she was shopping for a particular item, and when she said no, he descibed the different goods they carried.

Sarah walked around the shop fingering the luxurious gloves, shawls, and dresses and hats by Worth, the French couturier, but the counter that kept drawing her back was the one featuring French perfumes. The clerk hastened to let her smell the various scents offered. One that smelled of gardenias, made her smile with pleasure. She purchased the bottle and hurried back into the hotel with it clutched in her hand.

At the appointed time, she walked into the lobby dressed in her green silk dress and wearing the pearl combs in her up-swept hair. The aura of the gardenia perfume surrounded her with the smell of summer. She anticipated a magical evening at the celebrated restaurant with the famous actor. She hardly noticed Surratt waiting for her.

"Mrs. Slater, I have a cabbie waiting at the curbing if you're ready to leave," Surratt inquired.

Sarah nodded with barely suppressed excitement. Booth was waiting for them at the restaurant entrance. He immediately stepped forward to assist Sarah from the buggy, leaving Surratt to follow behind. As they entered the restaurant, he pointed out the columns at the entrance commenting they were reputed to have come from the ruined city of Pompeii. Sarah gazed up in awe as they walked past. When they entered the restaurant, the maître d'hotel greeted Booth by name, welcomed him back, and collected their wraps and handed them to a uniformed woman. As he led them to their table near the center of the room, every head turned to stare at Booth and the beautiful woman at his side. Sarah lifted her head with pride. In her silk dress with the pearl combs in her hair and Lottie's pearls at her neck, she knew she had never looked better nor had she ever felt more elegant and admired.

She studied the menu the waiter gave her as Booth explained that Charles Ranhofer was one of the greatest chefs of his day…guaranteeing the quality of any dish she might order, although the restaurant was most famous for its steaks. Sarah was mesmerized as his sonorous voice listed the notable personages that had dined there: Jenny Lind, Mark Twain, Charles Dickens, Edward I…Prince of Wales at the time, and Napoleon III of France. He added, of course, that he himself was a frequent diner along with other contemporary notables. He pointed to the decorative confectionery centerpiece on the table representing Queen Victoria and Prince Albert and explained it was called a piéce montée and was not meant to be eaten. Sarah thought to herself that she would not have dared spoil it anyway by attempting to eat something so lovely.

Sarah returned to the hotel feeling like someone walking on air. The Camden House Mansion, the Metropolitan Hotel surrounded by shops filled with goods from Paris, and the Delmonico evening revealed to her what a vastly different world existed beyond the one she had lived most of her life. Sarah was amazed that only a few months past she had been stuck on a farm in Salisbury wearing old, faded clothes and despised by her in-laws who treated her more like a servant than a family member. Now she was wearing silk, hobnobbing with the rich and famous, staying in an elegant hotel, dining with John Wilkes Booth, and carrying a purse heavy with gold.

John Surratt was sulking when they left New York the following morning bound for Washington. She supposed it was because he had been ignored the night before. That was part of it. Unknown to her, prior to her arrival, Booth, Atzerodt, and Surratt were bemoaning the failure of their plan to kidnap

Lincoln six days before when the President changed his itinerary and spoke at the National Hotel instead of the hospital. Surratt would not have been worried, but frightened if he had known that Wiechmann, smelling trouble, had asked the clerk in his office, Daniel Gleason, what to do with the information he had. Gleason relayed Wiechmann's story to his roommate, First Lieutenant Joshua Sharp, who worked with him in the office of Provost Marshall of the Army, Colonel Timothy Ingraham.

Sarah and Surratt arrived in Washington on March 25th at 7:30 in the morning. Surratt hired a four-seater carriage pulled by two white horses. He then drove them to his mother's boarding house. She came out of the house carrying the slippers Sarah had left behind, climbed into the rear seat of the carriage, and they drove off bound for Surratt's Tavern where Gus Howell was to meet Sarah.

SURRATTSVILLE, THE HOME OF JOHN H. SURRATT.—[Sketched by A. M'Callum.]

Surratt's Tavern, Surrattsville, Maryland,
courtesy the Surratt Museum

The news was bad when they arrived at the tavern to learn it had been raided the night before by the Federal Calvary. Howell was arrested by the commanding officer, Sergeant Seaton, leaving Surratt with the problem of arranging Sarah's transportation through Maryland. Surratt was terrified by the near miss. Had Seaton waited until that morning for the raid, he would have snared them all. While they sat at the tavern debating what to do, an old friend, David Barry walked in. He introduced Sarah as Mrs. Brown, an alias she was using on the trip. A visibly shaken Surratt explained his problem, and Barry agreed to help. Barry joined them for the drive to Port Tobacco after first dropping Mary off at her home. He left Sarah and Surratt at Brawner's Hotel in Port Tobacco, noted for being a nest for blockade-runners. Barry drove back to Washington where he returned Surratt's hired gig to Howard's Livery.

Sarah and Surratt spent the night at the hotel, after arranging to be rowed across the Potomac to Mathias Point the following morning. When they reached Mathias Point, Surratt explained the situation to Lieutenant Cawood at the Signal Camp who arranged a horse and buggy to carry them to Milford. From there, they took the train to Richmond arriving on March 29th. In Richmond, Surratt registered as John Sherman at the Spottswood Hotel where Sarah was also staying.

Richmond was in turmoil as Federal forces surrounded the city with a network of trenches that reached all the way to Petersburg. General Robert E. Lee had struggled during the eight-month long siege of Petersburg to hold off the Union armies, but he was slowly losing the fight. Should Lee, Commander of the Army of Northern Virginia, fail to hold Petersburg and the vital railroad connection there, it was just a matter of time before Richmond would fall to the overwhelming power of the Union armies.   Judah Benjamin, ever the realist and recognizing the end was upon them, collected a fortune in gold, necessary documents, and instructions before putting them in a large trunk with a concealed bottom. He then summoned Sarah to his office and hired her to return to Montreal with the trunk he provided. After she left his office, Judah Benjamin, a man with a unique sense of humor, sang a ditty he had composed called "The Exit from Shocko Hill."   He went home that night and began packing essential clothes and personal documents.

On April 1st, with barely time to catch her breath, Sarah was again bound for Canada. As she sat on the seat that bore them away from Richmond, Howell grumbled that Sarah must have done a lot of shopping in Richmond to need a larger trunk and to fill it to the point he could barely lift it. Sarah also wondered why it was so heavy, but, as long as she was being paid so handsomely, she was not going to question Secretary of State Benjamin's arrangements.

The White House, Jefferson Davis Residence, Richmond, Va.

As Sarah and Surratt traveled north, they left behind a doomed city. The following day, April 2nd, 1865, Davis and his entire cabinet fled Richmond on the Danville Richmond Railroad that General Lee was struggling to protect until they could escape. Behind them the fires that Davis had ordered set to destroy the arsenal, and other buildings of use to the conquering army, quickly spread to surrounding buildings consuming more and more in its voracious appetite. The burning city seemed to be spiraling into the skies on a black cloud lit by a myriad of glowing cinders that rained on the hapless heads of fleeing citizens.

Davis and his Cabinet would stay in Danville, the temporary Capital of the Confederate States of America for a week, before abandoning it and fleeing to Greensboro, North Carolina. When they reached the city, Generals P. G. T. Beauregard and Joseph Johnston advised Davis the situation was hopeless. With rail lines cut, Davis and the others traveled by horse, except for the heavy-set Benjamin who refused the indignity and rode in an ambulance as they traveled south. They stayed in Charlotte until the end of April as the two sides negotiated the terms of surrender. Leaving Charlotte, on May 2nd, they reached Abbeville, South Carolina. Benjamin pragmatically reassessed Davis's plan to flee to Texas. In Benjamin's opinion Davis, who had a $100,000 bounty for his arrest, would never make it before he was caught. Judah Benjamin found the prospect of arrest unpalatable. His decision made, Benjamin cheerfully explained to the others that he had decided to go his separate way, saying he was bound to "the farthest place from the United States, if it takes me to the middle of China."

In the meantime, Sarah and Surratt reached Leonardtown,

Maryland, without hinderance, arriving in Washington on April 3rd around four in the afternoon.   Surratt left Sarah at the Metropolitan Hotel on Pennsylvania Avenue to return to his mother's home for a brief visit. There he collected fresh clothing and exchanged some of the gold coins he carried for greenbacks with one of his mother's boarders, John T. Holohan. While he was preparing to leave, his mother's servant told him that a detective had been to the house looking for him, thus spurring him to even greater haste. Louis Atzerodt, his roommate and cohort in the attempt to kidnap Lincoln, cornered him in their room to ask what was going on, where Booth was, and what was happening. Surratt told him he had no time to deal with his questions as he had to get Mrs. Slater to Montreal. John kissed his mother and sister a hurried farewell and returned to the Metropolitan Hotel to check in for the night. He and Wiechmann went out for an oyster supper leaving Sarah to dine alone in the hotel.

The following morning, Sarah and Surratt caught the early train for New York. She returned to the New York Metropolitan where Surratt told her she might have to go on alone.   She thought nothing of it, as she had the previous times as well. Sarah checked into her room determined to examine the trunk she was transporting.   Removing her belongings and tossing them onto the floor, she reached the bottom of the trunk. Something seemed off about it.   Picking up a stocking, she used it to measure the inside dimensions of the exterior of the trunk and those of the interior. The interior was three inches shorter. Excited, Sarah began to search for a way to lift the bottom and see what was hidden beneath in the secret compartment. It took ten minutes of prying to work it up and lift it to one side. When she saw what had lain concealed, she gripped both sides of the trunk to keep from toppling in. Before her glittered a fortune in gold coins along with documents addressed to Thompson and Lee in Montreal. Shaking at the discovery, she carefully replaced the bottom and smoothed it down so the men in Montreal would not realize she had tampered with it.

NOT THIS TIME
Chapter 14

As she had done on her previous trips to New York, Sarah went to see her mother. While she waited for Antoinette to answer the door, she could hear her coughing. The door swung open to reveal her mother in her nightgown despite it being mid-morning.

"Are you unwell, Maman?"

"I have been plagued by this cough for over a week now. I can't seem to shake it. I didn't expect to see you again so soon. What exactly are you doing to be in New York so frequently? Are you living here?"

"No, I don't suppose I'm really living anywhere at the moment."

"So, what are you doing to keep coming to New York and giving me twenty-dollar gold pieces? You've not become a light-skirt, have you?"

"Of course, not. I have too much self-respect for something as tawdry as that. Remember, you raised me a good Catholic girl. I have not forgotten the catechisms of our faith."

"I'm glad to hear it." Antoinette stepped back, "Do you want to come in?"

"Yes, but I can't stay long."

Antoinette laughed before responding, "You never do. But then who am I to complain? Your brothers have never bothered to come."

"I am sorry. Have you still heard nothing from Eugene or

Robert?"

"Nothing. I know Robert has my address else he could not have given it to you. I pray nightly to hear that they are both well."

"As do I. Maman, as I said I cannot stay." Sarah reached into her purse and extracted two gold pieces. "Use this $40 to get some medicine and some coal. This room is like ice. You need to stay warm if you want to get rid of that cough."

"Thank you, Sarah. I know you think me cold and unfeeling, but I have always loved you and your brothers. I appreciate what you have given me more than you can know."

Reaching out to wrap her mother in her arms, she had tears in her eyes. She could not remember the last time her mother had told her she was loved. Sarah sniffed back the tears as she told her mother goodbye. The trunk with the gold was waiting to be delivered to Montreal.

Surratt, valise in hand, was pacing the lobby when Sarah returned to the hotel. He blurted, "I'm not going any further with you despite orders from Mr. Benjamin to escort you all the way to Montreal. I need to look out for myself now. John Wilkes is about to do something crazy. I am already under suspicion because of my association with him and something we tried to pull off. It failed, but that doesn't matter. We tried and apparently someone knows it. Mrs. Slater, you could be under suspicion for your association with us, so you are better off without me."

How dare they implicate her in their schemes. Sarah bit back anger as she retorted, "I don't know what you are talking about, John Surratt. I have no idea what you men have been up to…and you know it!"

"It's better you don't know what we were doing. I'm just warning you to watch your step."

Surratt was also carrying dispatches for Montreal, and he would deliver them but without Mrs. Slater. He had tossed restlessly the night before, mulling over the risk that his association with Booth and the others in the cabal represented to his life. He could travel faster and safer unencumbered by her.

Sarah had not realized he was supposed to go all the way to Canada with her until he informed her that she would be going on alone. Maybe, it also had something to do with the trunk, she thought. Was there something illegal about all that gold? Sarah looked Surratt in the eyes as she stated, "I did the trip to Montreal alone last time. I can do it this time as well."

He turned on his heel without answering and left. Sarah looked at his retreating back and wondered what had him so spooked. The Yankees already suspected him of being a courier, but what else was he involved in? And what was Booth planning that had Surratt running like a scared rabbit?

Leaving that night, Surratt arrived in Montreal on April 6th. When he delivered the documents to Brigadier General Lee, he was ordered to go to Elmira, New York, to determine the feasibility of having Confederate prisoners released from the notorious Elmira prison. He left immediately for Elmira, but under an assumed name.

With the Confederacy dying and Davis on the run, the Confederate office in Montreal was in turmoil as the men there pondered their own futures. Thompson's wife had arrived with $200,000 in British stock certificates. The Thompsons went undercover following Canada's order for Jacob's arrest. Edwin Lee was trying to hold it together, but when the Confederacy fell on April 7, it was a matter of time before he would have to look to saving his own hide.

Sarah's plan to leave on April 5th was thwarted when she awakened with a high fever. For a week and a half, she never left her room. The hotel room service kept her in hot tea and toast during the first week as she suffered through a severe case of flu. For the next few days, she was able to keep down beef broth and toast. Although weak and shaky, she dared not delay any longer. Rising from her sickbed on the 15th, Sarah dressed in her black widow's weeds. Before lowering the veil to hide her face, she looked in the mirror and recoiled in shock. The woman that stared back at her was a hollowed eyed shadow of herself. Her face had thinned from days with little food and her hair was lank and dull. Sarah shrugged her shoulders and used the contraption that allowed her to signal the front desk for a porter. When he arrived, he hefted her trunk and followed her down to the lobby. When she reached it, she looked around in alarm at the people that were racing around shouting that Lincoln had died.

Turning to the porter, she asked, "Oh, dear God, what happened to President Lincoln?"

"You haven't heard?" he exclaimed in shock. "He was shot last night at Ford's Theater. He just died. They are searching now for his assassin, John Wilkes Booth."

"Oh, no. You mean John Wilkes Booth, the famous actor?" Sarah could not keep the shock from her voice.

"Yes. They are also looking for John Surratt. He's accused of attacking and nearly killing William Seward, Lincoln's Secretary of State, while Booth was shooting Lincoln. Both are damned murderous traitors. They'll hang for sure if they're caught. Washington is already tracking accomplices according to the newspapers. Anyone involved with Booth and Surratt is going to hang, too. You mark my words."

As the porter talked, Sarah could hear the people around them baying for blood to avenge Lincoln's assassination. Sarah's pallid face blanched even whiter behind the black veil. She needed to hide, to escape, to do something to save herself. She was innocent of Lincoln's murder, but could that save her? Listening to the anger around her, she doubted it. What was she to do? The answer came to her. The past three months of traveling for the Confederate government had taught her vital skills that were now more useful than ever.

She was leaving alright, but not for Montreal. Not this time…

CAST OF CHARACTERS
Chapter 15

Sarah, Photo courtesy of Jane Clancy

SARAH SLATER

Born on January 12, 1843, in Middletown, Connecticut, Sarah Antoinette Gilbert Slater's trail disappeared in New York City in April 4, 1865. Over the years there have been various theories as to what happened to Sarah and the Confederate gold she carried. Did she leave for fear of being implicated in the murder of Lincoln or for some other reason? Was she a part of the cabal that plotted to assassinate him? With the Confederacy at an end, did she not know what to do with the gold...or to whom to give it? Did she keep the gold entrusted to her when the Confederacy failed? Did she join her brothers in France or in the Caribbean where they had relatives on both sides of the family, or did the three of them remain in this country? Are the real answers all lost in the vagaries of time? See the next chapter for theories of what happened to Sarah Slater.

Status: vanished?*

EUGENE FRANCIS GILBERT

Eugene Francis Gilbert was born July 14, 1836. He moved to Kinston, North Carolina, in 1858 and worked as a jeweler there prior to moving to Goldsboro in the winter of 1860-1861. He joined the Goldsboro Volunteers in 1861 with the rank of Sergeant and was among the occupying force for the former United States defensive fort, Fort Macon on Bogue Banks, a barrier island on the North Carolina coast. He was cashiered on November 29, 1863 in Goldsboro and tried for encouraging men to desert the Confederate forces. Eugene was pardoned by Robert E. Lee and moved to a camp near Kinston. He then deserted with his brother Robert. Supposedly, they were headed for New Bern 29 miles away. There is no record that he and

Robert ever arrived there. If they had joined the Union army stationed in New Bern or were taken prisoner there would be a record to that affect.

Status: vanished?*

ROBERT JACKSON GILBERT

Robert Jackson Gilbert was born December 8, 1837. Prior to moving to Kinston in the fall of 1860, he practiced as a dentist at 165 Market Street, Hartford, Connecticut. In the winter of 1860-1861, he and Sarah moved from Kinston to New Bern. He joined Company I, Second North Carolina Infantry, on May 29,1861. Rising to the rank of First Lieutenant, Robert was respected as a soldier at the time he attended his brother's trial in Goldsboro. Both Robert and Eugene ended up in a camp near Kinston following the trial, probably the camp at Wyse Fork, where they deserted. Wyse Fork was the eastern most Confederate defense of that part of the State. The land from there to the coast had been in Union hands since the Spring of 1862.

Status: vanished?*

* (note discrepancies section)

FREDERICK GODWIN GILBERT

Frederick Godwin Gilbert was born 1845. He moved to Kinston with his father and siblings and lived there in Nunn's Hotel until he, his father, and Eugene moved to Goldsboro in the winter of 1860-1861. On March 15, 1863, he enlisted in Company D, Thirteenth Battalion of the North Carolina Infantry with the rank of Private. He died of natural cause on June 6, 1863, and was buried at St. Stephen's Episcopal Church, Goldsboro. He was seventeen years old. (More soldiers died of disease during the

Civil War than were killed or died of wounds. Measles was particularly rampant, as was dysentery. Although there is no official record of the cause of death, it is likely that he caught an infection while serving in the army.)

ROWAN SLATER

Rowan Slater, born in 1835 in Rowan County, North Carolina, was the son of the esteemed owner of a large plantation. He married Sarah Gilbert on June 12, 1861. He and his brother James attended Trinity College where both excelled in music, but it was Rowan who pursued a career in dance and violin. In the early months of the war, he worked for the Confederacy in Goldsboro. Later, he enlisted in Company A of the Twentieth North Carolina Infantry. On April 6, 1865 he was captured in Farmville, Virginia and imprisoned. On June 26, 1865, he took the oath of allegiance in Newport News and was released.

After he was released from prison, Rowan returned to his family home in Salisbury. They were less than welcoming, condemning Rowan as the black sheep of the family. Eventually he left Salisbury and began life as an itinerant instructor of music in a series of rural communities, a career that left Rowan in extreme poverty in the stricken southland where such things as music lessons were a rare luxury. His family stopped answering his letters pleading for help.

Alone, sick, despairing, he found himself in Arlington, Virginia in 1881. On September 1st of that year, he replied to a letter from his brother James, then a successful retail merchant in New York City who had heard a rumor concerning the wife he had not seen since 1864.

"You wrote me that you heard that Nettie (Sarah) was dead. I hope she

is in a better world. If you have any of the particulars about her let me know. Of course placed in the situation that I am it is natural that I wish to know all, when did she die, where and under what circumstances. Give me all the particulars so far as you know."

Rowan's brother James Slater married a native of New York, sired a daughter, and lived in New York City until retirement. He then moved to live with his daughter in Winston-Salem, N.C. He died there in 1912 at eighty years of age never knowing if his sister-in-law, Sarah Slater, was in truth deceased. There is no record of Rowan's date and place of death.

MICHAEL CAMPBELL

Sarah Gilbert lived with the Michael Campbell family when she first went to Kinston until she and her brother left for New Bern. Campbell was a buggy maker in Kinston, a town noted for its coach works. His home was on the corner of Bright and Independent Streets.

JOHN LOUIS PENNINGTON

John Pennington, born May 28, 1827, in New Bern, Craven County, North Carolina (conflicting sources state he was born in Wake County) began a career in journalism working in Raleigh for the "Raleigh Star." In 1856, he moved to Columbia, South Carolina, and founded the "Columbian" newspaper. Although the details of the wedding are unknown, at some point he married Kate A. (last name?).

Ardent supporters of the arts, they moved to New Bern in 1858 when he became the editor of the "Daily Progress." While Sarah was living with the Penningtons in New Bern, John and his wife introduced Sarah to Rowan Slater. Pennington joined the army in September of 1861, but due to poor health, his service was brief. When he was mustered out, he returned to Raleigh and edited a newspaper by the same name as the one in New Bern. Following the war, he served for a time as state senator in Alabama.

Named governor of the Dakota Territory in 1874, his first wife and possibly their daughter had died, and he was remarried with three children, ages 12-16. His first love, however, was newspapers and he again started a newspaper in the Dakota Territory following his time as governor. Pennington moved in his later years to Oxford, Alabama, where he lived with his daughter Lulu, her husband Alex Adair, and their six children. He died in July of 1900 and is buried in Oxford.

JUDAH PHILLIP BENJAMIN

Judah Benjamin, a Sephardic Jew, was born in St. Croix in the Danish West Indies on August 11, 1811. He rose to Secretary of State under President Jefferson Davis. With the fall of the Confederacy, Jefferson and his Cabinet, including Benjamin, fled Richmond in April of 1865. They established a temporary Capital in Danville, Virginia, but fled a week later through North Carolina and into South Carolina hoping to make it to Texas to avoid capture. Benjamin, assessing their slim chance of reaching Texas, parted from Jefferson Davis and others of the Cabinet in South Carolina. He made his way south riding part of the way in a hired carriage pretending to speak only French. Although he had earlier eschewed riding a horse due to his girth, at some point Benjamin was forced to switch to horseback in order to reach the southwest coast of Florida. There a blockade runner, Captain Archibald McNeill, assisted him in reaching Bimini. Chartering a sponge boat to carry him to Nassau, he took to sea only to have the boat blow up. He survived, was rescued, and managed to make it back to Bimini where he persuaded Archibald to take him to Nassau. From Nassau he made his way to Havana, Cuba, before sailing for England on August 6, 1865 with a bounty of $25,000 on his head.

He arrived in Southampton on August 30, 1865. He spent only a week in London to help wind up Confederate affairs, before leaving to see his wife and daughter in Paris. With most of his property in the States confiscated, Benjamin wrote articles and practiced law to support himself. From time to time, Jefferson Davis visited him in London, but they were never again close.

As he aged, his health rapidly declined. Diabetes, a severe fall from a tram, and a heart attack in early 1884 presaged his death in Paris on May 6 of that year. He was buried in Père Lachaise Cemetery in his wife's St. Martin family crypt, following the Catholic rites she had arranged for this Sephardic Jew. It was not until 1938 that a plaque bearing his name was mounted on his grave. Although accused of purloining Confederate gold in London for his own use, considering his reduced circumstances, that is unlikely.

JEFFERSON FINIS DAVIS

Born on June 3, 1808, in Christian (Fairview) County, Kentucky, to a military family, Davis was one of ten children. Most of his growing up years were spent on Rosemont Plantation near the town of Woodville, Mississippi although he returned to Kentucky to attend the Bardstown boarding school. After Bardstown, he matriculated at Jefferson College, Mississippi, prior to transferring to Transylvania University in Kentucky. President James Monroe appointed Davis to a cadetship at West Point Military Academy in 1824. He graduated twenty-third in his class four years later.

From 1828 until 1835, Davis fought in various Indian campaigns. In June of 1835, Davis married Sarah Knox Taylor, daughter of his commanding officer, Zachary Taylor, future President of the United States who opposed the marriage causing Davis to resign from the military. Three months later, Sarah Taylor Davis was dead of malaria. Davis became a cotton farmer and soon was embroiled in politics. In December of 1845, he was elected to the U.S. House of Representatives. At this time, his remarriage to Varina Howell secured his place among the 'planter class' of Mississippi.

The years 1846 and 1847 found him serving in the Mexican-American War where he won nationwide acclaim under his former commander, General Zachery Taylor, who declared that his deceased daughter, Sarah, was "a better judge of a man than

I was." In 1847, Taylor appointed him Senator for Mississippi following the death of Senator Jesse Speight. Davis completed Speight's term and won re-election holding the seat until 1851 when he ran for governor of Mississippi and lost. He returned to public service in 1853 when President Franklin Pierce appointed him Secretary of War. He served in that capacity until 1857 when he again won one of Mississippi's senate seats. When Mississippi left the Union in January of 1861, Jefferson Davis resigned his senate seat and left Washington to go home to Mississippi.

Jefferson Davis served as President of the Confederacy from February 18, 1861, until May 10, 1865, when he was seized by Union forces near Irwinville, Georgia. Charged with treason, from May 22, 1865 until May 13, 1867, he was imprisoned at Fort Monroe, Virginia. Ironically, it was the abolitionist Horace Greeley who paid a portion of his bail to effect Jefferson's release from prison. Following his release, he declined an offer to serve as president of Texas A&M University, living out his later years in his beloved home, Beauvoir, on the coast of Mississippi. In 1881, he published *The Rise and Fall of the Confederate Government* to defend his politics. Jefferson Davis died of acute bronchitis on December 6, 1889, around one in the morning. Temporarily buried in Metairie Cemetery in New Orleans, his body was moved to its present location in Hollywood Cemetery in Richmond.

JAMES ALEXANDER SEDDON

James Seddon, who served as Jefferson Davis's Secretary of War, was born July 13, 1815. Due to a frail constitution, Seddon was taught at home and became self-educated. He entered the University of Virginia at the age of twenty-one to study law. Seddon served Virginia in the United States congress from 1845 until 1851 when ill health forced him into retirement at his plantation home, Sabot Hill, on the James River near Richmond. Jefferson appointed him to his Cabinet where his twenty-four months of service made him the longest serving of the Confederate Secretaries of War. He died on August 19, 1880.

JOHN WILKES BOOTH

An idol of the American stage and the heartthrob of thousands of adoring female fans, Booth was born on May 10, 1838. Some said he was the "handsomest man in America" and "a genius... possessed of an excellent memory." At the peak of his career he was earning the then astronomical income of nearly $600,000 a year. His parents were the renowned Shakespearean actor, Junius Brutus Booth, and Junius's longtime mistress, Mary Ann Holmes, an English immigrant. The ninth of ten children born to the couple, John Wilkes entered the world in a four-room log house on a farm near Bel Air, Maryland. In 1851, Junius's wife Adelaide Delannoy Booth granted a divorce to her husband on the grounds of adultery. Junius at long last married John Wilkes's mother, Mary Ann, on his thirteenth birthday. John Wilkes's brothers, Edwin and Junius, Jr., joined their father on the stage. Following in his brothers' footsteps, John Wilkes made his stage debut under the early pseudonym J. B. Wilkes in Richmond on August 14, 1855. He performed only once with his family, brothers Edwin and Junius Booth, in *Julius Caesar*, on November 25, 1864, at New York's Winter Garden Theater.

A skilled athlete, Booth excelled in horsemanship and fencing. Despite his intelligence, he was a lackadaisical student. While in school, a gypsy fortune-teller foretold a grim future and early death, saying he "would meet a bad end."

Strongly pro-slavery, Booth joined the Richmond Grays and was present at John Brown's hanging at Harper's Ferry on December 2, 1859. With the outbreak of war, Maryland was torn between pro and anti-slavery factions. Booth found himself increasingly at odds with some of his family who were pro-Union, particularly Edwin. Although Maryland remained in the Union, the state enacted legislation that was problematic in a border state. This action forced Lincoln to suspend the writ of *habeas corpus*, declare martial law in Baltimore, and station Federal troops in Baltimore and along the southern border. Booth was infuriated by Lincoln's actions which he considered unconstitutional. His increasingly inflammatory remarks against Lincoln and the Federal government led to his arrest for treason in early 1863 while performing in St. Louis. He was released after swearing the oath of allegiance.

PRESIDENT ABRAHAM LINCOLN

With the increasing battlefield losses for the South in 1864 and the re-election of Lincoln, Booth was pushed to ever more aggressive action. Through his secret fiancée, Lucy Lambert Hale, daughter of New Hampshire Senator John P. Hale, Booth procured tickets to attend Lincoln's second inauguration on March 4, 1865. In the audience were Lewis Powell (alias Payne or Paine), Louis Atzelrodt, John Surratt, and David Herold…a loosely gathered band of fellow southern sympathizers recruited by Booth to kidnap Lincoln. The group frequently met at the boarding house owned by John Surratt's mother, Mary Surratt. Booth learned that Lincoln would be attending a play on March 17, 1865, at a home for invalid soldiers on the outskirts of Washington. The game was on and Booth and his group were in place and ready when their plot was foiled. Lincoln changed his plans at the last minute. Atzerodt, seeing he was in over his head, began drinking more than customary.

Not only was Atzerodt worried at Booth's ramped up radicalism, but Surratt also grew alarmed by the loose cannon Booth posed. With the fall of the South, Booth realized that any further plans to kidnap Lincoln were useless. The new plan would be the *coup d'etat*: Booth would assassinate Lincoln. Atzerodt was assigned to murder Vice President Andrew Johnson, and Lewis Powell was to kill the ailing Secretary of State, William H. Seward. Herold was responsible for procuring horses from the livery owner James W. Pumphrey. Booth's friends, Samuel Arnold and Michael O'Laughlen were persuaded to join the cabal. Surratt was not involved in Booth's murder plot as he was in Canada on a mission for Judah Benjamin. With the three top government officials dead, Booth hoped to throw the Union into chaos. On Thursday, April 13, Lincoln gave an impromptu speech from the White House window declaring his support for freeing all slaves. His resolve hardened, Booth declared that Lincoln had just delivered his last speech.

Ford's Theater

April 14, 1865, Booth went to pick up his mail at Ford's Theater and was told that Lincoln would be attending the play *Our American Cousin* that night. Booth decided the time was ripe for putting his plot into action. General Grant was also to attend and sit with the President...a bonus for Booth. But Grant's wife insisted on going to New Jersey to visit family instead. Therefore,

Grant escaped being assassinated along with Lincoln. While the play was in progress, Booth peered through the peephole in the door of the President's box to assure that Lincoln was truly in attendance. Booth then entered the box and with his .41 caliber Deringer, shot Lincoln in the back of the head. When Major Henry Rathbone, who was in the box with the Lincolns, attempted to apprehend Booth, he was stabbed. Booth then leaped down to the stage declaiming *sic semper tyrannis*, "death to all tyrants." He and Herold then escaped on the horses waiting in the alley behind the theater.

It was midnight when Booth and Herold arrived at Surratt's Tavern, nine miles away on the Brandywine Pike. There they collected a stash of weapons secreted in the tavern. The plan was to escape through the swampy, heavily forested Zekiah Swamp area in southern Maryland, cross the Potomac and flee into Virginia where Booth anticipated he would be hailed as a hero. At some point on the trip, Booth's horse tripped in the dark. Booth was thrown and his leg pinned under the horse. In need of treatment for a broken leg, they fled to the home of Dr. Samuel Mudd, some twenty-five miles from Washington. In the small hours of the morning, the two men left Mudd's house and galloped off to the farm of Samuel Cox arriving around 4:00 a.m. on April 15th. Cox's foster brother, Thomas Jones, headed spy operations in that area of Maryland.

As Booth lay hidden in the woods while waiting to cross the Potomac...miserably uncomfortable with pain and the rough conditions, the nation plunged into deep mourning. Jones took him newspapers as he waited. On April 20th, he read that Mary Surratt, Powell, Arnold, and O'Laughlen had been apprehended. The prime culprit, Booth had a $100,000 bounty on his head.

Across the country, those who had treasured photos of Booth, ripped them from their albums and threw them away. Booth's name would live in infamy, not glory.

While Booth hid out, on the 21st, the train bearing Lincoln's body left the Washington station for a 1,662-mile journey through seven states. In the cities where the train halted, one half million waited to view his coffin. It was reported that another seven plus million people lined the tracks on route to see the train as it carried Lincoln on his final journey home to Springfield. At Mary Todd Lincoln's request, he was buried in Oakridge Cemetery in Springfield.

Garrett Farmhouse

Herold and Booth's two attempts to cross the Potomac were failures. Desperate, they sought refuge in a barn two miles south of Port Royal owned by Richard Garrett. The 16th New York Cavalry Regiment, under the command of Lieutenant Edward P.

Doherty, pinned them down in the barn. Herold gave himself up when the barn was torched, but Booth refused to come out. Without authorization to shoot, Sergeant Boston Corbett fired at Booth. The bullet lodged in three of Booth's neck vertebrae, severing his spinal column, and paralyzing him.

Three hours later, at the age of 26, Booth died on Garrett's porch where he had been dragged. The date was April 26, 1865. His body was removed to Washington and identified by family members based on appearance, a distinctive tattoo on his hand reading JWB, and a scar on his neck. He was then autopsied. He lies buried in an unmarked grave in his family's plot in Green Mount Cemetery in Baltimore.

Unwittingly, Booth's final act of revenge had doomed the south to far more severe penalties than it would have endured had Lincoln lived.

OLIVIA FLOYD

Olivia Floyd, a lamed spinster with southern sympathies, assisted Gus Howell and others in relaying information, supplies, and persons through Port Tobacco, Maryland. Her home, an imposing mansion called Rose Hill, was on Blue Dog Road. Reputed to be haunted by a murdered blue dog, Rose Hill was occupied by Union soldiers early in the war. Olivia charmed them with her wit, ghost stories, and gracious hospitality. Olivia could be feisty. She warned them, "Leave my fences and livestock alone, you Yankees, or I'll put ten of you in hell in five minutes." With two pistols always on her person, they likely believed her. Their Yankee tongues loosened by her generously poured champagne, she gleaned useful knowledge that she relayed to Laider's Ferry on the Potomac where waiting agents would relay messages across the river and to the necessary Confederate recipients.

In November of 1862, Edwin Stanton...Union Secretary of War, ordered her arrest and incarceration in the Old Capitol Prison in Washington when one of her messages was intercepted. The order from Stanton was never executed. She continued her activities and was critical in the relaying of information from Canada to Richmond following the capture of the St. Albans raiders.

The colorful little woman lived alone in the big house following the war and her mother's death. She became a practitioner of seances and told fortunes. Her doctor eventually shut down Olivia's lucrative practice as injurious to her health. He was aided and abetted by her priest. Olivia died on December 10, 1905, at the age of 81.

JAMES (HENRY OR A.?) FOWLE

Son of an Episcopal clergyman, James was involved in transporting Sarah Slater through southern Maryland. Implicated during the Lincoln conspiracy trial, he pled innocent to any knowledge of the assassination plot and swore he had never met Booth. He admitted to knowing both Gus Howell, Sarah Slater and Louis Atzerodt, and assisting them in traveling through southern Maryland.   Although questioned extensively by the military tribunal conducting the trial, his confused answers proved unhelpful in the prosecution's effort to prove Olivia Floyd and Sarah Slater were the same people.

GEORGE ATZELRODT

J. W. ATZEROTT.

Atzelrodt was born in Germany, July 12, 1835, and immigrated to the United States with his parents at the age of eight. Retaining a pronounced accent and not intellectually gifted, he never became fluent in English. As a young man, he started his own business repairing carriages in the town of Port Tobacco, however the business failed to thrive. It is likely that he met John Surratt in Port Tobacco, a hotbed of blockade runners. With the failure of his business, he relocated to Washington, and it was there that John Surratt possibly introduced Atzerodt to John Wilkes Booth.   In the trial of the conspirators in Lincoln's assassination which began on May 1, 1865, Atzerodt admitted to participating in the failed plot to kidnap Lincoln. However, he failed to carry out Booth's order to kill Vice President Andrew Johnson.

LOUIS J. WIECHMANN

Born in Baltimore, Maryland, in 1842, the son of German parents, Louis attended St. Charles' Seminary at the age of 17. It was there that he met follow student, John Surratt. Wiechmann and Surratt both left seminary without a degree and became lifelong friends. Louis roomed with the Surratt's in their boarding house following his employment as a clerk in the War Department in Washington. Wiechmann became aware of the conspiracies around Lincoln when John Surratt, forbidden by his mother to join the Confederate army, pursued his sympathies for the south through blockade running and becoming involved with Booth's plot to kidnap Lincoln. (The term blockade runner was used to refer to both ships and their captains and to agents of the Confederacy that transported people, messages, or materials across Union lines.)

As a firsthand witness to the goings-on in the Surratt house, Wiechmann's testimony was instrumental in convicting Mary Surratt, David Herold, Lewis Thornton Powell, and George Atzerodt and in their subsequent sentence to be hanged for conspiring to murder Lincoln. In his testimony to the Military tribunal, Gus Howell charged Wiechmann with providing military secrets to the Confederacy gleaned through Wiechmann's job clerking in the War Department. Although initially indicted as a conspirator, the charges against Wiechmann were not pursued. There was wide speculation that Secretary of War Stanton was leaning on him for a testimony favorable to the prosecution in exchange for dropping the charges. Others more charitable said that when sworn to tell the truth, he was forced by his conscience to do so.

Largely based on his testimony, many judged Wiechmann harshly when Mary Surratt was hung. He suffered deep remorse for the remainder of his life that he had brought about the death of a woman that had treated him like a son. Hoping to relieve some of the stigma attached to his name, shortly before his death on June 5, 1902, Wiechmann reaffirmed the veracity of his testimony in an official affidavit.

VICE-PRESIDENT ANDREW JOHNSON

The night of the assassination, Atzelrodt checked into the Kirkwood House, the hotel Johnson used as his Washington residence. Lacking courage to follow through on the killing, he instead began drinking in the bar of the hotel. He left the hotel well soused and walked around the city before fleeing to his cousin Hartman Richter's house in nearby Germantown.

The Kirkwood House bartender contacted the police after Lincoln's assassination and said Atzerodt had asked where Johnson was. The police searched Atzerodt's room at the Surratt house and found his bed unused the previous night. They discovered a hidden Bowie knife, a loaded pistol under his pillow, and Booth's bank book, damning evidence that proved his association with Booth.   Atzerodt was then arrested at Richter's house.

Atzerodt claimed that Booth knew he lacked the courage to kill Johnson and had assigned him as a back-up to assure that David Herold would kill the Vice President. He said he did not know anything about the plan to kill Lincoln until two hours before; however, he did admit to his earlier involvement in the plot to kidnap Lincoln. Atzerodt was found guilty of conspiracy to murder and was hung on July 7,1865, along with Mary Surratt, Lewis Powell, and David Herold, at the Old Arsenal Penitentiary in Washington.   He is buried in Glenwood Cemetery in Washington, D.C.

LEWIS THORNTON POWELL

Born in Alabama in 1844, Lewis Powell and his family moved to Florida when he was fifteen.   When the war broke out, Powell joined the Confederate army and would fight at Gettysburg where he was wounded and taken prisoner.   While in the war hospital in Pennsylvania College, he became involved with a volunteer nurse, Margaret Branson. It is likely that Margaret enabled his eventual escape from prison. Making his way to Virginia, Powell joined Mosby's Rangers. It was while he was serving with the rangers that he was commissioned to serve as an agent for the Confederate Secret Service.

He moved in with Margaret Branson at her boarding house in Baltimore. Claiming to be a deserter from the Confederate army, Powell took the oath of allegiance under the alias Lewis Paine. In Baltimore he teamed up with other secret agents: John Wilkes Booth, John Surratt, and David Preston Parr.   Booth then embroiled Powell in the plot to kidnap Lincoln.

When that plan failed to come to fruition, Booth assigned Powell the task of murdering Secretary of State William Seward as a component of the Lincoln assassination plot.

DAVID EDGAR HEROLD

One of eleven children and the only male to survive childhood, David Herold was born in 1842 in Washington, D.C.   His father, Adam Herold, as a Chief Clerk at the Washington Naval Yard, provided his family an affluent lifestyle.   Attending top schools in Washington, including Georgetown College, Herold earned a pharmacology degree.   To his detriment, while in college he met radical elements that would lead to his downfall.

An acquaintance of John Surratt, it was Surratt that would introduce him to John Wilkes Booth.   It was Herold that guided Lewis Powell to William Seward's home, before leaving to meet Booth in the alley behind Ford's Theater following Lincoln's assassination.   Escaping with Booth, they were caught at the

Garrett farm where he turned himself in and was brought to trial. Despite Herold's admission of involvement in the earlier kidnap plot, his lawyer tried to portray him as someone who had been duped by the savvy Booth. Herold was found guilty of colluding to murder Abraham Lincoln, Vice President Johnson, and Secretary of State Seward, and was hung with his co-conspirators.

WILLIAM SEWARD *Secretary of State,*

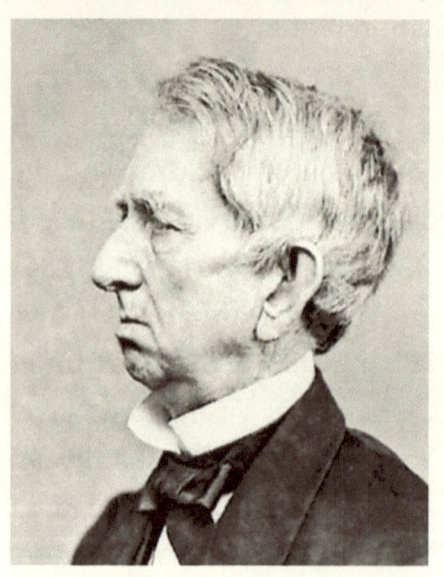

Seward was in bed suffering the aftermath of a recent accident when Powell arrived at his door pretending to be delivering medicine. Powell attacked Sewell's son and bodyguard on his way to stabbing Seward. The bodyguard recovered enough so that, with the help of two others, he prevented a mortal wound to the ailing Seward who would survive the stabbing. Powell escaped but was arrested three days later, tried, and sentenced to be hung with his co-conspirators, July 7, 1865.

AUGUSTUS NOLAN HOWELL

Gus Howell was born in Charles County, Maryland, in 1837(?). Prior to joining the Confederate army in Fredericksburg on June 25, 1861, he ran a tavern in the small community of Aquasco, Maryland. He was discharged from the First Maryland Flying Infantry, July 16, 1862, in Richmond, Virginia due to health issues.

The reason cited was Phthisis (tuberculosis). He immediately became an active agent for Confederate underground operations in southern Maryland, escorting mostly female agents and spies. In Baltimore, he hooked up with John Wilkes Booth who was also working for the Secret Service. He was arrested October 24, 1862 and charged with transporting men from Maryland to join the rebel army and was paroled.

Swearing the oath of allegiance to the Union, Howell was released from his second arrest which occurred around January 29, 1863, in Prince George's County, Maryland. He declared he could "stomach any amount of them (oaths of allegiance)." Wasting not a moment, he resumed underground activities until arrested March 24, 1865, at Surratt's Tavern, Surrattsville, Maryland. Gus Howell was incarcerated in the detested Old Capitol Prison in Washington at the time of Lincoln's assassination.

Winter trip

Called to testify at the trial for those involved with Lincoln's assassination, his testimony was less than helpful in providing information about the mysterious courier variously identified during the trial as Mrs. Slater, Mrs. Brown, or Miss Floyd. On August 8, 1866, Gus married Susanna Reynolds and went on to sire five children. He was a farmer, but unsuccessful, which forced his property to be sold at auction. He then became a laborer on a farm in New Castle, Delaware. Sometime before 1882, the Howells moved back to Maryland and became tenant farmers. In poor health the last years of his life, Gus and Susanna relocated near Elkton, Maryland, to live with his son John. He died in 1920 and was buried in Charlestown, Maryland.

JOHN HARRISON SURRATT, JR.

John was born on April 21, 1844, to John and Mary Surratt. He attended seminary but did not obtain a degree. Following college and after his father's sudden death, he took over his father's job as postmaster in Surrattsville, Maryland, where his family owned a tavern. After the elder John Surratt died, the family moved to their Washington townhouse, where his mother opened a boardinghouse. Although a southern sympathizer when the war broke out, Mary Surratt convinced her son not to enroll in the Confederate army. Still determined to serve, he became a blockade runner for the rebels escorting

Sarah Slater for a portion of her missions. It was not until December 23, 1864, that Dr. Samuel Mudd introduced Surratt to Booth. Booth convinced him to help him kidnap Lincoln for hostage until the Union released thousands of Confederate prisoners of war. The plot failed, and with it, Surratt saw Booth becoming more reckless as the fortunes of the South became increasingly dire.

On the day Lincoln was assassinated Surratt was in Elmira, New York, on a mission for Brigadier General Edwin Lee who had newly taken over Confederate operations in Canadian. When he learned that Booth had killed Lincoln, he fled to Montreal and then to St. Liboire, Quebec, where he was harbored by Father Charles Boucher, a Catholic priest. With a warrant out for his arrest as a co-conspirator, he was in hiding there at the time of his mother's death believing that the U.S. would not hang a woman. With Edwin Lee's aid, he fled Canada for Liverpool where he briefly stayed in a Catholic church. He next went to Rome and, under the alias John Watson, was hired by the Vatican as a Pontifical Zouave guard. Recognized by an old friend, who notified the U.S. minister in Rome, Surratt was arrested and imprisoned. He escaped and was befriended by Garibaldi who helped him escape to the Kingdom of Italy. From there he went to Egypt, but again was recognized and extradited to the U.S. to stand trial.

Unlike his mother's military tribunal, he was tried in civilian court on the charge of conspiracy to murder Lincoln and found not guilty. It was ruled a mistrial when the verdict came in eight innocent votes to four guilty. Under the statute of limitations, the time for charges other than murder had expired and he was released.

He worked as a farmer, then teacher, before a time as a lecturer. Following the collapse of his lecture tours he returned to teaching. Surratt married his second cousin, Mary Victoire Hunter, in 1872 and sired five children. At some point after his marriage, he gained employment with the Baltimore Steam Packet Company where he eventually rose to the position of treasurer of the company. Surratt died of pneumonia in Baltimore on April 21, 1916 and was buried at the New Cathedral Cemetery in Baltimore.

MARY SURRATT

Mary Jenkins Surratt

Mary Elizabeth Jenkins was born in Maryland in the 1820's. A devout Catholic, she married John Harrison Surratt in 1840 and had three children: John Harrison Surratt, Jr., Elizabeth Susanna

(Anna) Surratt, and a third child who did not survive. Her husband died unexpectedly in 1862 leaving her with an estate to manage and large debts. She rented the tavern in Surrattsville where they had been living to John M. Lloyd and moved into their Washington townhouse. To make ends meet, she converted it to a boarding house.

It was there that she met Booth, Atzerodt and others that would later tie her inextricably to the assassination conspiracy by dint of association. Although she steadfastly maintained her innocence, Wiechmann's testimony that members of Booth's band regularly met at her home was damning. Mary was further incriminated when Lloyd testified that Booth had given her a pair of binoculars to take to the tavern in Surrattsville for Booth to pick up later.

The verdict to hang her, the first woman so punished in the history of the United States, was and still is controversial due to many irregularities in the trial. Secretary Stanton held antipathy towards Catholics, didn't much care for women, and was eager to bring the conspirators to a speedy end. Civilian trial by military tribunal as he ordered was outlawed the following year. Mary was hung on July 7, 1865, despite a recommendation by five of the nine members of the tribunal for clemency. Stanton was suspected of concealing the recommendation while President Andrew Johnson was signing the papers for the hanging of the conspirators.

JACOB THOMPSON

One of nine children, Jacob Thompson was born in Leasburg, North Carolina, May 15, 1810, to parents, Nicholas and Lucretia Van Hook Thompson. His family enjoyed prosperous circumstances as a result of his father's business acumen and his mother's inherited wealth. He received his early education at Bingham Academy before matriculating at the University of North Carolina. Following graduation, he served for a short period on the university faculty. Despite his parents' hope that he would join the ministry, he had no interest in doing so. He left his position at the University in 1832 to study law and was admitted to the bar two years later. His first legal practice was in Pontotoc, Mississippi. Quickly becoming prosperous, Thompson soon owned three profitable plantations and made his home near Oxford.

In 1840, the gregarious and warm Thompson was swept off his feet by the beautiful and much younger only child of the wealthy planter, John Peyton Jones. Catherine (Kate) was only fourteen when he married her. Reluctantly, her father agreed to the union on the stipulation they wait to consummate the marriage, and that Thompson would pay to educate her in France and build her a suitable mansion in Oxford on land he purchased from a Chickasaw Indian. The smitten Thompson agreed to it all. Following her French education, Kate returned to the States two years later to begin married life. The following year, she bore the first of two children, a son named Macon. The family moved to Washington when he was elected as a congressman from Mississippi, a seat he held from 1839-1851. He lost the 1851 election and returned to the practice of law in Mississippi, having declined the opportunity extended by President Pierce to serve in the consulate in Havana, a plum post. In 1857, shortly after he took office, President James Buchanan appointed Thompson Secretary of the Interior. With growing northern antipathy to the slave-holding southern states, Thompson found himself in an untenable position. He resigned his position with the Department of Interior, and upon the declaration of war, joined the Confederate army. He fought in the battles of Shiloh, Corinth, Vicksburg, and Tupelo, attaining the rank of Lieutenant Colonel. In March of 1864, he was commissioned by Jefferson Davis to operate the Secret Service Office in Canada. He began his duties there in May of that year. While he was in Canada, his home in Mississippi (*Home Place*) was burned to the ground by vengeful Union troops. Making his base of operations at the luxurious St. Lawrence Hall Hotel in Montreal, Thompson found himself less than successful in attempts to free Confederate prisoners just over the Canadian border in Ohio, along with various other activities meant to be disruptive to the Union. His tenure in Canada came to an end with the failed St. Albans raid, and facing arrest in Canada, he and his wife fled to England where they resided for several years. Cited as a co-conspirator in the Lincoln assassination, the federal government posted a $25,000 reward for Thompson's capture. They returned to Oxford when it was safe to do so, but with their palatial home burned, they soon moved to Memphis, Tennessee.

In his later years, he became a benefactor of the University of the South in Sewanee, where he served on the board. In the last twenty years of his life, he fought to affirm his innocence of any knowledge of the Lincoln assassination plot and of stealing the Confederate gold held in Canada and London. His own substantial wealth, along with vast land holdings, and the fortune his wife inherited were more than sufficient for their affluent lifestyle...obviating the need for Confederate gold. Jacob Thompson died March 24, 1885 and was buried at Elmwood Cemetery in Memphis.

FACTS AND DISCREPANCIES
Chapter 16

Known Facts and Plausibility

The dates of Sarah's birth and that of her siblings is known. We also know her family heritage, connection to the Caribbean, and birthdates. There was an older sister named Josephine Elizabeth, born in 1833, but she was either married or no longer living with the family in 1858 as she is not included in the census for that year.

Sarah moved to Kinston, North Carolina, as cited, lived with the Campbells and then moved to New Bern where she lived with the newspaper publisher John Pennington and his wife. There is no record of what employment Sarah or Robert had, but one assumes there was some motive for the move from Kinston to New Bern. The scenario I have used is an attempt to explain the relocation. The Penningtons did have two newspaper apprentices living with them in 1861. John Pennington introduced Sarah to her future husband, Rowan Slater, son of a prominent family with a large plantation near Salisbury. The facts of Rowan's life are as presented in this book.

Sarah and Rowan married in Goldsboro and lived there until sometime in 1863 prior to moving to Rowan's home near Salisbury. He enlisted in 1864, leaving Sarah on the family farm. In early January of 1865, fed up with life in Salisbury, Sarah left Rowan and his family behind and went to Richmond for a pass to New York to live with her mother. The two Senators from

North Carolina in their letters of referral recommended she be given the pass.

Instead of moving to New York, she was hired first by the Confederate Secretary of War Seddon and then by Secretary of State Judah Benjamin to carry messages back and forth to Canada. Her beauty, fluency in French, wit, and daring were positive attributes for a courier. The messages she carried were related to the St. Albans raid, difficulties in Canada resulting from Confederate activities conducted from there, and the disposition of Confederate funds in the face of the growing certainty of defeat. She made three trips to Montreal, Canada and was paid in twenty $10 gold coins for each trip. In Montreal she stayed at the St. Lawrence Hall Hotel, the Confederate headquarters in Canada.

She was also paid an equal amount by Jacob Thompson, in charge of the Confederate office, for two return trips to Richmond. $1000 in gold coins, with Confederate script worthless, represented a fortune. By the time of her third and final trip, Thompson had been replaced by Brigadier General Edwin Lee. There is substantial speculation that Benjamin had charged her with getting gold to Canada to keep it out of Union hands. The stories of Jacob Thompson and that of Edwin Lee are factual. At the time she made the last trip, General Joseph Johnston was fighting on in North Carolina despite Lee's surrender and the fall of Richmond which occurred after her departure for Montreal. The gold was intended for transport to London where it could be used to fund a resurrection of the Confederate States of America. Following the South's defeat, there is no documentation that shows what happened to the Confederate gold, either on route or that which was already in

England through Thompson's orders.

Blockade runners extensively employed the routes through southern Maryland beginning with the crossing from Mathias Point near Port Royal to near Port Tobacco as described. As a blockade runner, Sarah met many of the players in the Lincoln assassination conspiracy who facilitated the underground route from Richmond through Maryland and then to Canada: Gus Howell, Mary Surratt, John Surratt, James Fowle, Louis Wiechmann, George Atzerodt, James Wiltshire, and Lieutenant Cawood. Olivia Floyd was active in assisting blockade runners and was under the eye of nearby Union forces. She was familiar to Howell and assisted him with lodging those he escorted. There is no proof that Sarah stayed at Rose Hill, but it is not an unreasonable scenario. The same holds true for the William Pratts, owners of Camden House, and the Stones' house, Haberdeventure. The stories related to Rose Hill, Camden House, and Haberdeventure are factual. Both Sarah, and John Surratt on at least one occasion, stayed at the Spottswood Hotel in Richmond and at Brawner's Hotel in Port Tobacco. Sarah stayed at the St. Lawrence Hall Hotel in Montreal on her first trip. I assume she probably stayed on the second trip as well, although there is no proof that she did so.

On Sarah's last trip, there is an unexplained time gap of a week and a half that occurred before Lincoln's assassination. She was on the way to Montreal and would have been there well before the assassination. I created the flu scenario to explain the delay. Then, when she learns of the assassination, Sarah takes flight.

Sarah met Booth through Surratt, but there is nothing to point to her involvement in the Lincoln conspiracy. She was actively sought for questioning during the military tribunal following Lincoln's death, but no one could find her. Witnesses could not, with certainty, swear to her name, nor could they say what she looked like because of the heavy black veil she wore. She was variously identified by others as Olivia Floyd, Mrs. Howell, Fanny Brown (Booth's mistress), and Kate Thompson, among other names.

Questions and Discrepancies

George N. Sanders, a former journalist with extensive connections in both the U.S. and Europe, created the courier route from Richmond to Montreal and from there to London and Paris where agents worked to promote Confederate interests. They were well funded. With the end of the war, what happened to the Confederate funds they could access?

George N. Sanders

The Confederate government named the former U.S. senator from Virginia, **James M. Mason,** as envoy to England.

James M. Mason

John Slidell, former U.S. senator from Louisiana, headed the office in France. Married into a prominent creole family, it is likely that Judah Benjamin and Slidell were well acquainted. Not only was Slidell active in France, but he established an extensive network of spies in England.

John Slidell

John Wilkes Booth was a notorious womanizer. Rumored to be married to a woman named Izola D'Arcy, he kept her tucked away in the countryside while he pursued other women. The marriage was probably bigamous as she was already married to a Charles Bellows.

Izola D'Arcy

John fathered a daughter with Izola, Ogarita, who went by the last name Bellows. Ogarita would grow up to become an actress. The secret engagement to Lucy Hale may or may not be factual as there is some dispute about this. However, he was apparently smitten by her.

Fannie Brown, an actress, was a known mistress. There were legions of other women that fell for Booth. Were any of these women in on the plot to murder Lincoln?

Fannie Brown

The Mystery solved?

There are various versions of what became of **Sarah Slater,** confederate courier on the route George Sanders established. One states she was arrested in New York and held in Federal custody. There is no record of either a warrant for her arrest or of her release. If they had the real Sarah in custody, is it not reasonable to assume they would have most certainly brought her to trial…either as a witness or as an accomplice? Some sources state that the government was holding her surreptitiously to hide the Federal women spies that had infiltrated the Booth cabal. In his testimony, George Atzerodt did not mention her name but that of **Kate Brown,** a *Federal* operative that had infiltrated Booth's group along with two other women spies hired by

Lafayette Baker. Baker was the head of the Union Secret Service. If these women spies learned of Booth's intention to kill Lincoln, is that not sensational enough news for it to have been reported to the U.S. government officials concerned with protecting the President? There was antipathy between Lincoln and Baker after Lincoln shut down one of his operations. Was this enough to cause the egotistical Baker to look the other way when his spies reported the Booth Plot?

Lafayette Baker

According to recent research, to maintain Brown's secrecy, Sarah Slater's name was substituted as it would not do to have it known that Federal government officials were aware of Booth's plot. This ties in with an attempt to substantiate the claim that there were subversives in the Lincoln administration who promoted his assassination. One United States government employee, Charles Lee, was the first arrested; however, he was released by Stanton and disappeared. What political dissention in Lincoln's government would cause some in the Cabinet to not stop a known assassination plot from being executed? Were Stanton or some others unhappy with Lincoln's more lenient plan for dealing with the South…and dissatisfied enough to let Booth execute his plot?

Atzerodt's confession was stolen, but a copy turned up in 1977. Other evidence collected by authorities was buried, squelched, or was sealed until 1935 when sealed documents became accessible to researchers. Why? Was it to hide complicity? What documents disappeared? Why would they have been destroyed? The public did not gain access to the surviving documents until 2009. Was Sarah Slater merely a name thrown out as a red herring in a cover-up of a sinister collusion-to-assassinate-by-default?

Another version of her later years says Sarah divorced Rowan Slater in 1866 after failing to reconcile. It states she twice remarried to older men in poor health and was widowed when both predeceased her. Sarah was said to have trained as a nurse, thus explaining her marriage to the ailing second and third husbands. Sarah bore no children in any of the marriages.

According to the remarriage version, Sarah had a sister, Laura Louise Spencer, with whom she lived between her second and third marriages. Laura Louise Spencer is not listed among her siblings in other accounts (no mention of Josephine Elizabeth as previously noted until clarification by John Stanton). Since her parents went their separate ways in January of 1860, it is reasonable to assume they sired no other offspring, thus one might discount Laura Louise Spencer.

In this scenario, her purported will shows a good number of assets. It also says she owned property in Lenoir County, North Carolina, Kinston's location. It is doubtful that a recorded deed exists in the county records to prove ownership, as the courthouse burned twice prior to 1889, destroying county records unless purchased or deeded after the 1888 fire. Furthermore, when she stayed in Kinston, she would not have had the assets during that brief period to buy property. There is no record of her returning to Kinston, and in the Spring of 1861, she would have only passed through on her train journey to Goldsboro. Her family was also no longer in Kinston since they had relocated to Goldsboro in the winter of 1860-1861. One brother was dead and two were missing after November of 1863, and there is no record the two missing brothers returned to Kinston after they deserted.

If this is the same Sarah, there is no record according to family stories, that she ever mentioned any wartime activities. This Sarah's marriages can easily account for the assets in the will. A research of the old New England family of Gilberts shows at least a dozen Sarahs, and various Josephs, among other names of Sarah Slater's immediate family. Does this lead to possible confusion as to the real Sarah Antoinette Gilbert Slater?

According to another source, Sarah died in Poughkeepsie, New York, on June 20, 1920. The reputed tombstone for Sarah is off by twelve years on the birthdate, which can be explained by saying Sarah lied about her age. This gravestone bears the name Sarah A. Spencer (A. for Antoinette?) ...Spencer for her reputed third husband, William Spencer, whom she married when he was widowed by her sister Josephine's death.

Her "second" husband, Jacob M. Long, leaves no mention of a Sarah Slater, former wife, nor does any census show they ever lived together. That marriage certificate uses the name Nettie Slater, nee Gilbert. Sarah Antoinette Gilbert Slater was her legal name. Why would she have used Nettie on an official document? Was this a sham marriage created for the purpose of changing her name in order to throw investigators off her scent, as some have speculated? One document, said to refer to our Sarah Slater, lists her name as Nellie. Did someone forget to cross the l's? Another reputed gravestone for our Sarah Slater is in North Carolina. One is reminded of St. Constantine's mother returning from the Holy Lands with two heads of John the Baptist. Quite a feat that.

Poughkeepsie Rural Cemetery, N.Y.
(After photo by Patrick A. Teater, Sr.)

The obituaries also contain discrepancies. One states that her mother, Antoinette Reno (a possible mispronunciation of Reynaud which would have sounded like *Ray-no* in French), was born in France. Other sources state she was born in Trinidad.

Perhaps, the family was remembering the details of her life as best they could?

One of the more credible accounts is by John Stanton, historian with the Surratt Society, who states that brother Eugene moved to Florida and developed the land in Duvall County where Atlantic Beach and Neptune Beach are located. Buying the land for a pittance, he became a millionaire. According to Wikipedia, this Eugene Gilbert, *a jeweler from Connecticut*, was responsible for initially planning Atlantic Boulevard to connect Jacksonville to the nearby beaches sometime around 1890. Eugene is reputed to have given his siblings various plots of land. One in Kinston was said to have been given to Josephine Gilbert Spencer and was inherited by Sarah at her sister's death. If so, no record would exist in the courthouse in Kinston to verify the deed unless deeded after the 1888 fire.

Is this the solution to the mystery of Sarah Slater?

Mr. Stanton also states that Sarah's mother, Antoinette Reynaud Gilbert, died in Hoboken, New Jersey, where she was living with a Robert Gilbert. Buried in Hoboken initially, her body was later moved to the cemetery in Poughkeepsie to lie beside her daughters, Sarah and Josephine.

Are these various versions lies, mistakes, mistaken identity? Or does Mr. Stanton have the solution to the puzzle of what became of Sarah? And, that still leaves the question of what became of the Confederate gold…that which she was reputed to be carrying, not to mention those funds already in English banks?

I leave all these questions to the reader's discretion.

Bibliography

Books non-fiction:
Winkler, H. Donald, Stealing Secrets, Cumberland House, 2010.
Markle, Donald E., Spies and Spymasters, Hippocrene Books, 1994.
Stern, Phillip Van Doren, Secret Missions of the Civil War, Wings Books, 1987.
Books fiction:
Byrd, Max, The Sixth Conspirator: A Novel, Permuted Press, 2019.

Articles:
Lee, Charles, The cover-up of Booth's Unknown accomplices.
Hall, James O., *The Lady in the Veil,* "The Maryland Independent," July, 25, 1975.
Boyko, John, *Opinion: Confederates and Confederation,* Montreal Gazette, May 8, 2014.
Lewis, J. D., Map, *North Carolina Railroads, 1860,* N. C. Department of Transportation.
Brooks, Rebecca Beatrice, The Disappearance of Sarah Slater: Confederate Spy and Lincoln Conspirator, May 14, 2013.
Higginbotham, Susan, The Veiled Lady: Sarah Slater, Courier for the Confederacy.
Higginbotham, Susan, *History Refreshed.*
Stanton, John, *Some Clarifications on a Recent Article,* Surratt Courier, March 2016

Wikipedia Online Articles:
John Surratt
Mary Surratt
John Wilkes Booth
Sarah Slater
Louis Wiechmann
George Atzerodt
Lewis Powell
David Herold
Olivia Floyd
Jacob Thompson
Kate Thompson
Judah Benjamin
Jefferson Davis
James Seddon
John Pennington
Camden House
Haberdeventure
Rose Hill
Metropolitan Hotel, New York City
Port Tobacco
Port Royal
New Bern in the 1860's
Kinston in the 1860's
Lincoln Discussion Symposium: online thread November 6, 2015.

Photographs: most of the photos used are public domain, according to the Library of Congress guidelines as they were taken prior to 1924.

Persons and various buildings in the book, photographs courtesy of the Library of Congress.

Photos of Camden House, courtesy of the Library of Congress.

Metropolitan Hotel, NYC, courtesy of the Library of Congress.

Photo of St. Lawrence Hall Hotel, courtesy of the McCord Museum, Montreal, Canada.

Photos of New Bern, Courtesy of Jim Hodges, President, New Bern Historical Society.

Photos of Haberdeventure and Rose Hill, sourced on-line.

Photos of Surratt Boardinghouse and Surrattsville, courtesy of the Surratt Museum, a   division of the Maryland-National Capital Park and Planning commission.

Photos, Mathew Brady.

Photos of Sarah Slater in the text and on the cover, courtesy of Jane Clancy, photographer, Sunbury, Victoria, Australia. The right to use these photos is reserved.

Maps: created by James Martin Atwater.

About the Author

Betty J. Vaughn, former department chair and art teacher at Enloe Magnet High School in Raleigh, NC, launched a career as an author after leaving the classroom. She is the 2013 winner of the award for historical fiction from the North Carolina Society of Historians for her book *Run, Cissy, Run*. Previously her books *The Man in the Chimney* and *Turbulent Waters* won the awards for 2011 and 2012 respectively. *The Intrepid Miss LaRoque* is the fourth book in the series. The novel *Yesterday's Magnolia* is not part of the historical fiction series.

In honoring her books, in a unanimous decision, the judges commented: "It is gratifying to find an astute historian whose skills far exceed that realm; someone who can take facts and weave them together with fiction and end up with a story that actually could have happened...[It is] a wonderful story full of emotion, unexpected twists and turns, close calls and tragic moments...Mrs. Vaughn can consider herself a seasoned novelist...[Her books] are fast paced, action packed, and full of adventure...Her work simply isn't just a flurry of words, dry, and boring...She is a master of literary technique as she weaves together her tapestry of words."

A prize winning visual artist with paintings in collections worldwide, Mrs. Vaughn designed the magnet art program at Enloe where her students consistently won top honors. The recipient of a three year Federal Grant to the Wake County School System, she led Enloe Enterprises, Inc. in operating an art gallery, a summer arts camp, and an Emmy award winning television production company. As a result of the Enterprises Enloe was selected as one of the ten best art schools in the nation by Business Week Magazine. She wrote and published a monthly newsletter for the Enterprises and is the author of numerous professional articles.

She loves to travel and led study tours of Europe for many years. History, art, and books are a lifelong passion. Both as a teacher of advanced placement art history and as a writer, Mrs. Vaughn brings the story of the past alive through the people who lived it.

NC Society of Historians
Established December 1941

AWARD WINNER

"Vaughn's first book, MUDDY WATERS, was reviewed by our panel and selected as an award-winner in 2011. We reunited with memorable characters and were introduced to new ones as the saga continues in TURBULENT WATERS. The characters in this novel become real to the reader. We became swept up in the novel and didn't want to put it down until we had finished reading it. Vaughn captured the essence of the difficult reconstruction period. So smoothly did she work 'history' into the story, that we were taken aback at times when we realized the book was a series of 19th century life's lessons.

Vaughn can consider herself a seasoned novelist! Her work simply isn't just a flurry of words, dry and boring. She is a master of literary technique as she weaves together her tapestry of words to develop a picture that is complete, yet can be added to in the future. Each volume is self-sufficient but leaves the reader wanting more, hoping for more...and this volume is no different from the first in that respect.

This novel earns the 2012 Historical Fiction Award due to the unanimous decision of our panel."

--The North Carolina Society of Historians

Other Titles by Betty j. Vaughn

Title: *Yesterday's Magnolia*

- Paperback: 350 pages
- Language: English
- Hard Cover Book ISBN: 9781590955543
- Paper Back Book ISBN: 9781590955550
- eBook / ePub: ISBN: 9781590955567

Jo envies Margo and Maurice for their ready charm, looks, wealth, glamour, and exciting lives never realizing that it is she who is envied for a life that contains the things that they themselves long for and have not attained.

"It's a shame to have so damned much and yet so little." An eastern North Carolina farmer's daughter, Margot, streaks like a comet into the life style of the rich and famous. Her beauty and exuberant, zestful personality gain her entrance to boardrooms, the White House, a corporate jet stocked with Cristal champagne and caviar, a villa in Italy, and marriage to one of the world's most powerful men. Maurice, the spurned suitor, seeks friendship and comfort from Margot's sister, Jo, a quiet, bookish art history teacher. Jo envies them both for their ready charm, looks, wealth, glamour, and exciting lives never realizing that it is she who is envied for a life that contains the things that they themselves have not attained. Like the comets they so resemble both Margot and Maurice are consumed by the friction of life, leaving Jo to remember the magic moments they brought to a more conventional path.

Title: *Tiger's Code*

- Paperback: 256 pages
- Language: English
- Hard Cover Book ISBN: 9781590953907
- Paper Back Book ISBN: 9781590953914
- eBook / ISBN: ISBN: 9781590953921

Book One of a Quint Cord Novel

Quint Cord's latest assignment is proving to be his most challenging and could well lead to catastrophic events if he does not break the code in time to avert them.

Quint Cord is an unlikely spy. With sufficient family money so that he never needs to work, he could have spent his life idling on a beach, chasing women. But from the moment he discovers famous codes of the past in a university class, he is hooked. His unique talent for creating and breaking codes brings him to the attention of the CIA.

A powerful and ambitious politician, who's in cahoots with a Saudi prince, plans to seize the US presidency and throw the western world into turmoil. Quint flees the country only to stay one step ahead of a foe determined to kill him before he can break the code.

Clue by clue, Quint begins to zero in on his target but can he stop him in time?

Title: *Dragon's Sword*

- Betty J. vaughn
- Language: English
- Hard Cover Book ISBN: 9781590953808
- Paper Back Book ISBN: 9781590953815
- eBook / ePub: ISBN: 9781590953822
-

Book Two of a Quint Cord Novel

Quint Cord returns to the CIA when his fiancée is almost killed by an egomaniacal hacker who is determined to use his GPS satellite implanted virus to gain control of governments and transportation networks around the globe. Aided by a North Korean dissident who vows to bring down the Kim Jong Un regime, the hacker uses the North Korean's information to crash ships and missiles in Korea and Japan. The hacker next turns to his own country of China to create friction with the United States. When the North Korean becomes frightened for his life and defects, the hacker flees China for fear he will be exposed. Lila Carson, Quint's fiancée, is again on the trail of the hacker as he goes dark to elude discovery.

From North Carolina to Japan and China, and then to Seattle, Quint struggles to capture the man before he can commit more murder and chaos.

Title: *Lyon's Claw*

- Betty J. vaughn
- Language: English
- Hard Cover Book ISBN: 9791590958000
- Paper Back Book ISBN: 9781590955598
- eBook / ePub: ISBN: 9781590955604

Book Three of a Quint Cord Novel

Lila and Quint Cord are honeymooning in the south of France when Lila is kidnapped. Seized because of her hacking expertise, her captor plans to use her in a deadly game of revenge. While Quint and three CIA operatives work to free her, another and more dangerous plot unfolds with global implications. With hired assassins on their heels, Quint and the other agents must discover what secrets led to the enmity between Lila's captor and his nemesis, recover Lila, and stop the realization of a deadly plot.

Title: *Run Cissy Run*

- Paperback: 304 pages
- Language: English
- Hard Cover Book ISBN: 9781590956748
- Paper Back Book ISBN: 9781590956755
- eBook / ePub: ISBN: 9781590956762

Book One A Cecilia LaRoque Novel

You would think Cecilia LaRoque has it all: a loving father, wealth, beauty, social position and a devoted suitor. She doesn't. Crushed by a cold and critical mother who soon absconds to live with a dissolute lover, 'Cissy' struggles to prove herself worthy of love and respect. She could not have foreseen in her teenage years that the genteel and privileged life she had led would come to a crashing halt with the outbreak of Civil War, a bitter struggle that would tear her world apart. Despite the hardships and inherent danger, she seizes the opportunity to forge an unorthodox role for herself as a spy.

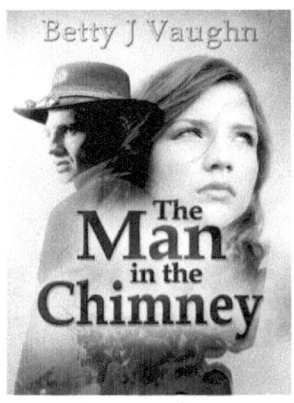

Title: *The Man In The Chimney*

- Paperback: 352 pages
- Language: English
- Hard Cover Book ISBN: 9781590956021
- Paper Back Book ISBN: 9781590956038
- eBook / ePub: ISBN: 9781590956045

Book Two A Cecilia LaRoque Novel

The War Between the States has come to eastern North Carolina, bringing hardships, pillaging, and fear to the local residents. For those left at home, the struggle to procure the needs of daily life is all-consuming; for those serving in the armies of both North and South, death is a daily companion. Against this backdrop, an unlikely and forbidden love affair between a local woman and a Union officer leads to difficult choices for them both—choices that will tear them apart and force them to deal with the abandonment of their dream of a life together.

Despite broken hearts, misunderstandings, and missed chances, Penny and Ryan strive to survive the dangers and ravages of war and make the best of their separate futures. With the surrender of the South at Appomattox, Penny realizes she has one last chance to either find the man she loves or settle for a life alone.

BETTY J. VAUGHN

TURBULENT
WATERS

Title: *Turbulent Waters*

- Paperback: 328 pages
- Language: English
- Hard Cover Book ISBN: 9781590951743
- Paper Back Book ISBN: 9781590951750
- eBook / ePub: ISBN: 9781590951767

Book Three A Cecilia LaRoque Novel

LOVE IS PERSONAL, WAR IS NOT, especially in North Carolina, 1865-1867, during the reconstruction. With a love they are certain will transcend all else, southern belle Penny Kennedy marries Union Officer and attorney, Ryan Madison, despite the condemnation of those around them. The initial days of wedded bliss end abruptly when Marcus, the man who courted Penny for years in anticipation that she would marry him, is arrested for murder, and Ryan is assigned to prosecute him. As hard as this development is to tolerate for Penny, she will discover worse things await her before Ryan and she can attain the life they desire.

Title: The Intrepid Miss LaRoque

- Paperback: 300 pages
- Language: English
- Hard Cover Book ISBN: 9781590957103
- Paper Back Book ISBN: 9781590957110
- eBook / ePub:: ISBN: 9781590957127

Book Four A Cecilia LaRoque Novel

When Wilmington falls in February of 1865, Cissy LaRoque no longer needs to spy. That will not stop her from finding a new career where she can prove her worth beyond societal expectations of a woman. With the war drawing to an end and Wilmington occupied, she is faced with desperate circum-stances. Ryan Madison, a Union officer from the past, and Brandon McLean, a new one, attempt to help her. While attracted to them both, she is aware of family and community hostility toward the enemy and dares not act on the attraction. Her fiancé, Logan who is fighting for the southern cause, does not arouse her ardor like the two Union men. When the Confederacy falls, she convinces her father to allow her to run his shipping office in New Berne while he maintains the main office in Wilmington. There she discovers Ryan has married and Logan has jilted her. Provoked and titillated by a man she cannot have but craves, she puts aside romance and concentrates on business. Despite her father's initial objections, much to his surprise she succeeds far beyond any expectation. Although she is happy in what she has achieved, she is frustrated by what she has lost.

www.ingramcontent.com/pod-product-compliance
Lightning Source LLC
Chambersburg PA
CBHW061615100726
47898CB00002B/665